WOOING AND WARRING.

A STORY OF CANETUCKEY.

WOOING AND WARRING

IN THE WILDERNESS.

BY

CHAS. D. KIRK

(SE DE KAY).

"LAND WHERE WE LEARNED TO LISP A MOTHER'S NAME—
THE FIRST BELOVED IN LIFE, THE LAST FORGOT."

Halleck.

NEW YORK:
DERBY & JACKSON, PUBLISHERS.
LOUISVILLE, KY.: F. A. CRUMP.
1860.

W. H. Tinson, Stereotyper.

Geo. Russell & Co., Printers.

TO

MY MOTHER

THIS VOLUME IS AFFECTIONATELY DEDICATED

AT HER SUGGESTION IT WAS WRITTEN; HER SMILES OF ENCOURAGEMENT CHEERED THE HOURS ALLOTTED TO ITS COMPOSITION, AND HERS WILL BE THE APPROVING WORD WHEN THE COMPLETED WORK IS PRESENTED HER—FOR WHEN DID A MOTHER, SUCH AS MINE, EVER FAIL TO SET THE HOLY SEAL OF APPROBATION UPON THE FAITHFUL ENDEAVOR OF HER BOY?

C. D. K.

TO THE READER.

THIS book does not aspire to the dignity of a Novel. Its pretence, if pretence it have, is to illustrate the domestic life of the early settlers of Kentucky, by a series of sketches of their manners and customs, somewhat rudely drawn, but with filial love and an earnest attempt at truthfulness. To preserve the unity of the work, a simple thread of family experience—mainly veritable—is introduced.

And these words are all the author has of explanation or apology, for his reader, here at the outset.

LOUISVILLE, *February*, 1860.

CONTENTS.

WOOING AND WARRING.

I.

A LOOK OUT TOWARD CANETUCKEY.

AMID the drear days of the second month, there shines, now and then, one whose warmth is like to that of May—a day when the sap flows in that most fair of our American forest trees, when the rich mold of the earth grows loose, when the first birds hymn stray waifs of song upon the home roof, and the cheek is fanned with the blest wings of the not far off Spring.

Such had been the day; but as it waned, and the shade of the elms grew in length, and the fresh wind made the air chill, in the west banks of black clouds were piled. A pall was spread over the scene. From the bare bough of a scarred oak a crow cawed its hoarse note of ill-bode. From the depths of the dark wood came the hoot of the owl. Than these, there were no other signs of life, with such still pomp did the Night march up to its throne.

See! In the flash of an eye the gloom is changed to gold. The sun, loath to leave the world, looks out once more with his great eye of fire. Back flee the clouds. The sky is bright and the earth glows with the kiss of these last rays. And there, in the far west, shines the star of eve! Venus! in all climes the star of Love and Hope!

Atop the gate, just in front of his snug Virginia home, sat Dobson Hardy. For more than an hour his eyes had looked out to the west. He had seen the change from sun to shade, and felt in his heart that thus had been his life. Once it was bright with smiles of joy and peace, and then came the dark hours of grief and tears. But, thought he, why not from these varying phases of nature take courage? Yon star of pure lustre and brilliant beam was born of the gathering gloom. In the same west may there not be a propitious planet whose radiant rays and gentle influences will dispel the fogs and mists and darkness of life's eventide?

Thus it happened that his thoughts were turned toward CANETUCKEY—then a dim land, lying far in the West, concerning whose cane-brakes, swift and deep streams, green plains, rich soil, blue skies, and groves populous with red foes and wild beasts and grim death, strange, wild and weird stories were told beside every hearth-stone in the Ancient Dominion.

In this mood of mind, Dobson would have spent hours, had not his dream of a good time to come been suddenly snapped by a rude twitch of his coat tail, accompanied by the sound of an Ethiop's voice:

"Mars Dob, Miss Jane wants you right off."

Good man, faithful husband as he was, down he got from his perch and walked straight to the house, quick to do as his wife would have him.

Just as he trod the first step of the porch, a form emerged from the shadow of a privet bush, and stood at his side.

"Good night, sir," said Dobson, holding forth his hand.

The grasp which the man gave him in return was not one of warmth, and the voice, in reply, was hollow and husky, as if from the grave.

Kind in deed, as in word, the host proffered

his strange guest the bowl carved from the soft buckeye, and handing him the pail of water, bade him wash. This, in those old days, was the first of the rites of hospitality. Both rinsed their brown hands and tanned faces, and then into the great room, bright with the flame of a wood fire, they went. Spread out before them was the evening meal. A cloth, white as snow, and food which Apicius would even have thought worthy his feast! At the head of the table, in the place reserved long ago by some wise pragmatic sanction, the wife appeared. Her black hair was streaked here and there with lines of grey, and her face, once smooth as the rind of a peach, was seamed with lines of care. But her eye gleamed with light and life, and her form, even with its matronly *embonpoint*, bore witness of the grace that marked the girl.

As her glance meets that of the strange man she starts, and her whole frame quakes with ill-concealed dread. She sees at once who it is that has thus burst on her sight, and her heart throbs as if it would break. Hard is it for her to say one word or even to nod the head in recognition. There is a storm in her breast, and to calm its rage all her strength must be used. With an ease that shocks her, and a look that wears the guise of innocence, he takes a seat at her table. Then Dobson and his queer guest fall to. The ham, and the cakes of corn, and the rich milk, and the tea of sassafras, and the maple molasses, make them feel that it is good with toil and long walks to whet their love of the full-heaped board. Talk there is, but it is small talk.

All this time Mrs. Hardy, strange as it may seem, holds her tongue!

But her eyes tell tales. Now they glow with fire and fury, and then her cheek pales and those fierce eyes are wet with tears.

Of the day that has been so fair, and of the farm and the prospective crops they talk. By and by the bairns, one by one, march off to bed, and there is left but the good man and his good wife, the guest and a girl, who, for more than a dozen years, has plucked the first June roses down by the brook-side. The beech log sobs and sighs, the sparks fly, the red coals glow. All is snug. But there are hearts ill at ease. The young girl, with the bloom of health upon each cheek, with a quarrelet of pearls in her mouth, with eyes as modest and meek and blue as the violets that will blossom after awhile in the unfrequented glade, with a high proud brow and a lithe shape, is, and she knows it not, as she sits toying with those auburn ringlets, the cause of this keen ache in the heart of Mrs. Dobson. In the man of black beard and gruff voice and strong limb, she has roused a sentiment that has long slept. Not love, but pride,—ay, pride mixed with hate.

All this while the master of the house sits in his chair, and smokes his pipe and dreams of a new home west of the Blue Ridge, where corn grows to giant height, and the only pests are Indians, catamounts and weeds. He recks not what stirs the breasts of those seated so near him. But he shall soon hear, for the moon is up and it is time for bed. The words "good night," are said, and Burkitt is shown where he is to lodge—a big bed where he might lose his big self in the world of soft goose-down with which it is stuffed.

II.

A MIDNIGHT INTERRUPTION.

"DO you know, Mr. Hardy, the man you brought here to-night?" asks the wife, when they had been left to themselves.

"Some poor fellow, foot-sore and way-worn, I dare say. But why do you ask, Jane?"

"Wretch that he is, why shouldn't I ask? I have a mind to go straight off and turn him out of the house. Vile, mean, contemptible rogue, spy and murderer, he should be swung from the nearest limb. And you don't know him? I saw through him, though his face was all beard. I should know his eyes of sin"—

Just then the noise of hurrying hoofs on the road, and a rough rap at the door caused Mrs. Hardy to cease in her sketch of their guest.

"Who's there?"

"A friend, Greene."

"What's the row?"

"We want a skulking spy, and you must help us."

At the words the wife threw open the door, and before them stood twelve men, armed *cap à pie.*

Their spokesman and leader, a bronzed, but open faced youth.

"The down was scarce upon his chin,"—SCHILLER.

briefly told them of Burkitt's appearance in the neighborhood that day.

"Burkitt," cried Hardy, with an ejaculation, which, though frequently used by ministers and deacons, could hardly be regarded as reverent at this crisis, and is consequently omitted from this page.

"Yes, and here he is, right in this house, in my best bed, the mean wretch!" screamed the wife.

It did not take long to verify what Mrs. H. had said. Two or three bounds and the men were beside the bed where their game lay. Deep sleep shut him out from all sense of fear, and it was not until a rude arm was laid on him that the smile quit his face, and the tiger, wakened from his lair, flashed upon them his eyes of fire.

That this was the man of whom they were in quest, all knew. Cords were brought, and Burkitt, bound hand and foot, was thrown upon a horse, his head hanging on one side while his feet were dangling in the air, his body only resting across the animal's back. To hang him there in the woods next to the house, and put an immediate end to the bad man, was their intention. But Mrs. Hardy, now that she had done what she could to rid her house of the spy, in a stern voice bade the men not hang Burkitt on her place.

"Take him to jail and give him the judge and jury."

The mob yielded to the determined will of the one woman, weak though she was, and strong though they were. Performing a mobbish deed makes cowards. A brave spirit, equipped with the virtues of moderation and justice, can put to flight half a hundred rioters.

With a rush and a roar, as if borne on the wings of the storm-fiend, they rode back and placed their prisoner safe in the log jail of Fauquier, C. H.

All of this was in the year of our Lord 1785.

III.

BIOGRAPHICAL.

DOBSON HARDY was in the ranks of the Virginia Continentals—Col. Thomas Marshall's regiment—six years. He tracked the snow with his blood at Valley Forge; he was at Trenton and Princeton; he lay sick with the small-pox, and nigh unto death, at Morristown, in the Jerseys; at Yorktown, the Bible, which he wore next to his heart through the whole war, proved a shield to ward off death; a bullet pierced the book more than halfway through, but was spent in force when it reached the page whereon that verse is inscribed: "For thou, Lord, wilt bless the righteous; with favor wilt thou compass him as with a shield."

You may see the old book yet in the hands of one of Dobson's heirs who lives in the north of Kentucky. It is a quaint volume, but quite as much the Word of God as if bound in sumptuous leather, with clasps of gold. And far more is it to be prized for its good, true, brave Saxon tongue, than are the new words which new men in these new times would palm off upon us in our Bibles.

Jane and Susan Merrill were the twin pinks of the Shenandoah Valley; born in that vale which still blends rich fields and bright streams and rude scenes—a piece of Nature's work with which Art could not hope to vie.

Jane was wooed and won by Dobson Hardy; Susan, by William Burkitt. Both husbands possessed neat farms in Fauquier. There they made their homes, blest with small stores and pleased to live the lives of poor, but just men.

The tea was thrown to the sharks in Boston harbor. Patrick Henry spoke to the verge of what the British alleged was crime and treason. Washington drew his sword beneath the old elm at Cambridge. The land heaved with the tumultuous throbbings of the pulse of Liberty. To be slaves or to be freemen, was the alternative. What could these two plain farmers do but choose the better part?

But, alas! In the first year of the war Burkitt was bought with the gold of the foe, and for months plyed the task of a spy. When his base sin began to be whispered about he fled to the camp of the British, and with their troops fought thenceforth. Cursed with words of gall by his former comrades, shunned by his new messmates, as one who had proven traitorous, racked with the pangs of his own conscience, the poor wretch led a life which he thought but the foretaste of hell.

To Burkitt's wife the intelligence of his crime was a blow which caused her reason to reel in its seat, which planted an agonizing thorn in her side, and sunk her heart to the depths of woe. It appeared as if she could not live. Her name was stained. Her hopes were all crushed. But a wife's love, when it is pure and strong and deep, as it was in this case, falters not. It finds food in woe—a source of strength in the bitter waters of Marah. Susan, though she knew the name of her husband was scoffed, still clung to him, and when, in the midst of the war, she heard he was with Arnold and his men in the southern counties, she set out one night to find him in his work of theft and fraud. Thereafter her days were hours on hours of sharp pains;

her nights, when sleep touched her lids, dreams of fright and fear.

War had made Burkitt a madman. The fond kiss with which he was wont to greet his wife gave way to kicks and cuffs; the words of love to oaths. Yet she was true to him. Mild, meek and bland in all her ways—to soothe his rough path and tame his wild heart, her sole wish and thought and aim.

IV.

THE VANITY OF ALL THINGS.

"I AM so glad that you did not hang that man!"

"What man?"

"Why, when you were all here that night I woke in such a fright, and, stealing quietly to the door, I saw the man as you took him from the house; and he looked at me with eyes so full of pain!"

"But he will be swung yet, as he ought to have been long since."

"Now, why need it be so? The war is at end. We have peace, are free, and why should more blood be shed? Why not spare this one, vile and base as he is? Let him live that he may blot out the sins of the past, by good acts in the future."

"You talk well, though your doctrine of

works is not orthodox; but you talk for naught."

"Oh, Basil, it is not in your nature to want blood, and I feel that you can and will surely stay the red hand which could strike this man, though guilt does load him down."

"Your tongue, Mary, is as sweet as the honey of Hymettus. It should not plead for those who have done so foul a wrong to the land of their birth."

"Well, scourge and brand him, and send him out into the world with a worse mark than that which Cain bore; but spare his life. Let him not be cut off in his sin."

"I shall think of what you urge with, such force and eloquence, but"——

"Oh, Basil, none of your ifs and buts. Mean and trite words, they ever stand in the way of good deeds. Now, this is the last time I shall ask you to please me—for years, and it may be for all time."

"Why, dear girl, what do you mean by talking in that strain? Don't I live to please you, and am I not continually striving to learn what will light up the eye and make glad the heart of my Mary?"

"Yes, yes, you have ever been very good to me," said the girl, with a gasp and sob in her voice. Tears came to her relief, but they were kissed away before they could leave a trace of sorrow, and each sigh was stifled by the fond encircling arms of Basil.

Thus, the love of the two did that for them which—according to Lord Bacon—marriage accomplishes. It halved their griefs and doubled their joys.

The whole plan was then unfolded to Basil—how the family intended moving to Canetuckey in the spring, and then came the thought that she scarce dared give words to—the thought that they were soon to part, it might be to meet never more this side of the fearful stream of Death.

Basil cheered her with his eloquent words of hope, and the promise that only one year should elapse until he would join her in the new home. Ah, how many maidens have fed upon promises—fed until they became skeletons in body and paralyzed in heart!

Down the walk these two strayed, arm in arm. No words now. But looks of love, and heart-beats, and hand-grasps, and lip-seals. Then, one gush from the soul—one clasp of breast to breast, and the proud youth leaps upon his horse and spurs down the hill and out of sight.

Basil Greene was two and twenty—a bold, compactly built, dark eyed, dark haired, high-browed young man. He had been raised to the plough; but it had long been his darling ambition to shine at the bar, and, for a year past, he had been reading law. Apt to learn, he had made such progress that in a short time he was to make his first speech in court. And then, thought he, the path to fame is broad and straight before me. Wealth can be grasped—what love prompts seized, and Heaven on earth will be mine.

Vain boy! Your aim has been that of scores and scores of bright, glad youth. Wealth, fame, home joys—these are the fruits of the Hesperides, for which we climb and strive, and toil, and wear out our hearts, and spin out our minds and starve our souls.

Who plucks them? Once, in the lapse of an age, you may chance to see a spare, bent, pale man, with thin locks and eyes from which joy has fled and steps from which youth's gait is gone, and he holds in his hand the apple of gold.

He has been sharp, and shrewd, and keen, and close, and mean, and false, and here, at the grave, while Charon waits his boat and the Styx rolls its black flood in sight, he hears himself called the man of wealth.

And there is one, who, step by step, has made his way up to the dizziest height of fame. His name is noised through the wide world—his word is law to the whole land; but his heart has grown cold as ice; his face is a lie, for it smiles with grace; his words are cloaks to hide thoughts of fraud. Through years he has marched, and crawled, and fought, and moiled, with feet in the mire, and hands at foul tricks, and heart with black spots, on the road to fame, which once lay before him so bright and broad.

And there—sight to fetch tears from heart hard as stone—sits the stricken old man, who once, as you do now, my boy, gave loose rein to love and hope. On his breast are scars as thick as if he had been in the wars of all the Cæsars. He has had his bouts with Cupid, the blind god being urged on by maids as false as fair. He has had his dreams of sweet trysts, of the ring and the altar, of a seat by the fire, of a face to grow the brighter at his coming, and children to rise up and call him blessed. Well-a-day! He has eaten the long-coveted fruit. It turned to ashes upon his lips. Yonder he sits by his desolate hearth-stone, and shivers with the drear winter of age as he mumbles over the names of the loved and lost, whose graves the pure snow is shrouding this bitter night.

V.

THE DEPARTURE.

HEARING that in Culpepper an Emigrant Society had been formed, with which he could unite, and thus make the trip to Canetuckey in greater safety, Hardy rode over to the adjoining county, and entered into the compact. He found quite a number who were like himself on the eve of a great change of home and home scenes. Of course the one topic of conversation was the new land in the golden West—

"A fairy land of flowers and fruit and sunshine,
And crystal lakes and overarching forests,
And mountains around whose towering summits the winds
Of heaven untrammelled flow—which air to breathe
Is happiness now, and will be Freedom hereafter
In days that are to come."

With these new made friends Dobson laughs, sips his dram, smokes his pipe, says smart things, and is the life of the crowd in the bar-room. But all this gaiety is mock—at heart he grieves, be cause of the step he has taken. Still he has gone too far to think of receding. His Fauquier farm has been sold, and the day is agreed upon for the start on the long and drear trail through the woods and wilds to the Canaan of their hopes, and it is high time that they are gone. The spring has come, and they will be too late to plant corn for this year's crop. But there are fields to be cleared and ploughed, and prepared for the fall wheat and the turnip patch.

At last the day came for their departure. It was March. Raw, bleak, chill. Here and there a patch of snow lay on the hill-sides and in the shaded hollows. The road was knee deep with mud. Not a bird was to be seen or heard—the creek was bank full—grey clouds shut out the sky from view—the trees had not yet leaved.

They stand in the midst of the desolate scene, upon the threshold of the old home—to them home no longer. As the door is closed, and the echo reverberates through the deserted house, they feel as if alone in the world. Tears rush to the eyes of husband and wife. Dobson, in haste, and half mad, for he thinks that it is not the part of a man to weep, brushes away these signs of emotion. But the wife allows her heart to flow out in tears; nor seeks to check their gush.

But we have no time to look back—no time to sigh and mourn. The best foot is put forth. It is now, march, march; on, on—through the sleet which now falls—there will be sunshine by and by;—through the mud and mire—there will be dry ways soon. Brave hearts keep up! Dry your tears—smile now—let us have a shout—clap your hands—one more cheer—there is the Court-house—crack your whip, Tom—spur the nags, boys—we must dash through, lest the folks see we are loath to leave them.

They jog on at a right good pace, but just as they reach the Court-house (by that name the Virginians were wont to call the towns at which their courts were held), they meet a large crowd. Just in front of the mob, for such it seems to be, there comes a man in a half run, with eyes down, back bare, and on his white flesh, still quivering, you can read two letters—D and S. The cursed brand has just been burnt in with red-hot steel, and the mob laugh at the agony of the wretch, and pelt him with stones and sticks, and worse yet, they jeer him with cruel words that cut his heart so that it bleeds, flint though it has been for years. No one need tell us that this is Burkitt. Mary's plea with Greene had saved the life of the spy. So the state was spared the cost of a rope, and the culprit the pain of a death choke.

As the fugitive passed the procession of movers they caught a glimpse of his face. It was black as night. The furies seemed to have set their seals upon each lineament. On Mary he cast a devilish leer, which caused the girl, weak as she was from the sad tasks of the past few days, to start with such fright that she would have fallen from her horse, had she not then and there heard a voice of cheer, and felt the grasp of a strong arm.

Oh how the words of those we love can bear up the faint heart—how a tone, if it comes through lips we have pressed to ours, is balm to the sore and sick mind.

It was not till near dusk that Basil Greene could say to Mary: "I must leave you here." His lips refused to utter a farewell:

> "For in that word—that fatal word—howe'er,
> We promise—hope—believe—there breathes despair."

All day they had been side by side. But we shall not write down what their hearts bade their tongues tell. We shall not say how they gave kiss for kiss in pledge of love. Nor shall we speak of that low wail, as if from a heart that was quite broken, when Mary saw the form of Basil disappear in a turn of the road.

Then the sun went out in her sky!

VI.

ON BRADDOCK'S ROAD.

WINCHESTER was at that day the chief place of rendezvous for those parties who took the route across the mountains to the West. Before the war it had been a brisk town, from the fact that near it was Greenway Court, the seat of Lord Fairfax.

Hardy found all his friends assembled, and saw that soon the plunge into the wilderness must be made. But the sight of the towering mountains, now so near, did not frighten him. He felt that he was gifted with a magic wand—Self-reliance—which he could wave, and level these obstacles with the plain. His years of calm ease; his days and hours of "don't care," were gone. His heart was full of new hope; his brain full of new thought; his hands itched to do great things.

By sunrise one morning the cavalcade of these pioneers was seen defiling out of Winchester, along the steep road that led toward the Alleghanies. It was a novel sight. Its like is not vouchsafed to us in these days of railways and steamboats. As an advance corps were a party of negroes, with axes and spades, prepared to make the way smooth. Then came the creaking wagons, well laden with household plunder, and containing portions of the family. From beneath the up-lifted linen covers, black eyes and blue eyes and grey eyes, set in heads red, raven and flaxen colored, peep forth. A low puling wail, such as denotes new life—life which knows but few yesterdays and may not have many to-morrows—is heard issuing from within; while a negro nurse, in the soothing language of babydom, quiets the young heir to adventure. Near by comes a gaunt, showily ribbed horse, upon which a colored woman sits. She rides with a jaunty air, as the poor animal lifts its weary feet, staring from her great white eyes upon every new object on the road-side, and grinning, with her ivory-filled mouth, at the antics of her boys—for she is the mother of that numerous progeny which acts as a body-guard to the stock.

You may observe the leader of the expedition bringing up the rear, though this seems a contradiction in terms. He bestrides a tall, muscular, but not graceful specimen of the equine race. He is primitive looking. Uncouth in appearance, but strong in purpose and mighty in deed. From his black eye there beams the uncontrollable will which has borne him successfully through many a perilous undertaking. Upon his sun-embrowned features there reposes a calm expression of confidence. In those iron sinews lieth the strength which lays broad the foundations and rears high the superstructure of empires. That rugged hand is alike capacitated to fell the forest and nurture the rose. It will be strong to smite the savage, and gentle to smooth the brow of pain.

To Fort Cumberland the road was wide and smooth, and each night they found a house where food and rest could be had. But after leaving that sentinel outpost, the way was full of perplexities—narrow, rugged and disheartening. It was the same wilderness path that the army under Braddock had travelled in the disastrous campaign of 1754, and there were hourly evidences in the blazed trees and the rotting stumps, and the relics of encampments, and the ruins of bridges, of this route having been the line of march for military squadrons.

How different the purpose of these half hundred souls who now struggled through morasses, up acclivities, across swollen streams, beside beetling crags, on the verge of dizzy precipices! Their destiny is one of peace—to conquer nature with the arms and arts of husbandry—to soften the wild features of the wide West—to plant flowers and reap harvests, and create home and happiness. No bugle blast heralded their approach—no measured tread gave notice of their march. There were no banners waving—no swords gleaming—none of the pomp and circumstance of glorious war. It was the tramp, tramp, steady and slow, but sure, of the advancing hosts of Civilization and Christianity.

VII.

THE ALLEGHANIES.

TO-NIGHT the guide promises the weary travellers they shall climb the last mountain range, and on the morrow see outstretched before them the great valley of the West.

Just at twilight the train halts, and in a sheltered nook where they will be protected from the rude mountain winds the adventurers fix their camp-ground. Near by sparkles a silver stream, the voice of which, musical and low, sings a gentle lullaby as it eddies about the aged roots of the huge monarchs of the forest, which here rear their crests skyward. Through the green arches broken gleams of moonlight fall upon the gathering groups. Green arches we say, for though it is the latter week in March, and there is snow upon the exposed cliffs, and a nipping frostiness in the air, still these larch and laurel, with their voice of thunder when the gale and the storm sweeps through them, are perennial in their greenness. Here, miles of toil and travel from the dull, monotonous plain—above even the clouds—next to heaven itself, they are clad ever and ever, through summer and winter, in their glad, green robes.

But hear the echoing horn. It calls the stragglers to supper. What a scene of brightness is presented! In the centre is the fire, shooting its tongues of flame high and wide, until all the woodland aisles start out distinct and warm. And there is a savory odor abroad on the fresh air. The wandering Soyers have already served a feast. Nothing dainty; nothing to cloy the appetite. Strong food for the muscles and sinews. Hot drinks to dispel the cold.

Hunger appeased, they cluster in groups around the fire. Of the day's adventures, of the morrow and what it will bring forth, and of the days yet to pass before they reach the long sought goal, they converse. Presently the children fall asleep, and soon the ground is covered with blankets, in which the hardy men and women wrap themselves to dream out the night:

Sub Jove frigido.

Now nothing is to be heard but the quiet step of the sentry, the loud hoarse breathing of some sleeper, and the snapping, crackling sound of the fire which throws its ruddy glare upon the strange and picturesque scene.

The good angel of Krummacher's parable, Der freundliche Engel des Schlummers, has mantled all those people in the folds of forgetfulness. They are oblivious to present toil and care and danger. To their closed eyes is vouchsafed a power of vision more wonderful than clairvoyant ever boasted. They see the whole range of past years; they enjoy the pleasures of youth; they roam the fields of childhood; they fish, they bathe, they are blithe boys again. They see their mothers smiling fondly on them; they catch the proud glance of their father, at their first manifestation of manly strength or manly tact.

And the power of the seer is granted them. They obtain glimpses of the future—they see glory and fortune shining afar off, and hear the siren voice of the tempter begging them to haste and seize the golden gifts.

Oh blessed sleep and blessed dreams!

Yonder rests Mary:

Her dewy eyes are closed,
And on their lids, whose texture fine
Scarce hides the dark blue orbs beneath,
The baby sleep is pillowed:
Her golden tresses shade
The bosom's stainless pride,
Curling like tendrils of the parasite
Around a marble column.

She starts. The fall of a dead leaf has half waked her, and she stares about, fancying strange terrors in the forest glooms which the fitful fire-light illumes. This is but for a moment. Slumber comes again, and when the noise and bustle of the camp at grey dawn disturbs her, she is disenchanted from the fairy-land where for hours she has been roaming.

Breakfast is dispatched. Horses are geared and saddled. Again the band moves on, and after a few minutes they have surmounted the ridge which, for so many days, has stalked before them a seemingly impassable barrier. Before them is now spread a scene calculated at once to captivate, dazzle and awe the mind of the beholder. Sunrise upon the Alleghanies—a sight once beheld, it is never forgotten—is granted them. They are in some measure a rude, uncouth and unlettered party; but the God of Nature has implanted in them a love of the grand and the beautiful, which is more true and appreciative than that cultivated dilettantism which is affected by the modern habitués of perfumed palaces.

The stars have already faded and vanished before the advancing light. The east is purple. Now the herald beams of the imperial sun blaze upward. The far summits are touched with the glow as if it were Heaven's own fire. The breezes, that have loitered through the night in fairy caves, awake, and lift the mists that hang over the deep valleys. From a hundred altars, on mountain slopes and in the wild, dark tarns, there arise wreaths of blue vapor, the incense of nature's votaries. How the world now stands revealed! What a succession of hill and vale and plain! Woods on all sides, save yonder, where in a narrow gorge you can see the sinuous course of the far river—see its meandering way only. Not the flashing stream—not the limpid water—not the clear, swift current—not the gentle flow—none of these, but where these all are. And over all this scene there reigns a silence as profound as that of original chaos. It is only when they release their eyes from the soul-subduing vision, that they perceive down, far down in the gloomy recesses of the deep valley, the flash of a waterfall, and hear its tinkling melody. And from this they are recalled by the loud flap of wings above them, and see an eagle in its circling flight hover one moment far aloft, and then balance his sharp talons and unsteady wing upon a bare crag, screaming with his fierce voice until the blue empyrean echoes his notes of war and conquest.

VIII.

FACILIS DESCENSUS.

IT was all down-hill now. Even the fagged horses and the weary cattle comprehended the change, and cantered along at a merry pace. Leaving the higher regions of ice and snow, the climate changed, and warm puffs of air came up the valleys—pleasant welcomings to the west of the Alleghanies.

Mary, wearied with almost incessant riding, and anxious to relieve her mind from its painful thoughts, gathered half a dozen of the merriest and maddest of the children for a romp along the road, which was now a soft, green sward. And there were flowers, too—the children of the forest—just awaking from their long sleep, and peeping forth from their leafy beds with the mild and beautiful eyes of gentle innocence, loveliness and truth. The fair girl did not long participate in the jollities of her young friends, although she herself had proposed them. She soon discovered a harmony between the aspects of nature and her own feelings. She felt as if the clouds and gloom that, since leaving Fauquier, had wrapped her soul in impenetrable melancholy, were about being dissolved. She could feel new and fresh blood coursing through her veins. She could feel a suffusion of pleasure upon her cheek. She knew from her elastic step and her leaping pulses and the proud arch of her neck, and the glad, hot tears that would come to her eyes, that she was a new being, with new hopes and new duties. Not that she forgot the gallant and handsome young lover over the mountains; not that she joyed in the prospect of freeing herself from the bondage of love; not that she imagined to herself new conquests she might make, other hearts she might entrap, other proud youth she might lead a wildering dance through the mazes of courtship. Oh no! The fetters which bound her heart were silken, of the softest texture, and yet of the strongest woof. Her heart bounded and made music in itself, because it was relieved of a weighty load of apprehension. The fear that she could not triumph over her own grief—the fear that she might give way to despair—that her heart might become an aching void, loving not—that her cheeks might fade and her eye dim and her form droop, and that thus, at the appointed time, she could present her betrothed with but the shadow of herself—all this fear and apprehension was gone; dissipated by the breath of the first spring morning in the West.

She loitered by the way. She plucked snow-drops and violets, and arranging them with that native taste for the beautiful which most women possess, she placed the artless bunch of flowers in her bosom, and sang a wild joyous carol, which went floating through the tangled passages of the lone woods, and woke the long disused pipes of a listening mocking-bird, who answered the young girl's strain with a multitudinous melody, like a rain of glossy music under echoing trees.

In an instant her voice is choked—she is blinded. She sinks in unutterable despair. Lost, lost. It may be forever from home and friends, but not from Heaven and God.

IX.

LOST.

"IT'S a' weel. But she was a bonnie lassie. Providence works in a mysterious way. I've thought all along she would have suited me precisely, when we reached the settlements. But I've no right to complain. Ken I not how the fairest, comeliest of Greenock lassies was sunk in the treacherous quicksands; and wadna' she gi' me a buss whene'er I listed. Ah, laddies, shall I tell you the sad story?"

"Not now, Campbell. The old folks might hear you, and it would be painful to them."

There was a general movement to escape from the vicinage of the wordy and windy Scotchman, whose stories were invariably long drawn out, but rarely composed of linked sweetness.

The children had soon wearied of their sports, and hastened forward to overtake the train, which was more than a mile in advance. They reported Miss Mary as coming on, but as she did not overtake them in a few minutes they halted, so that she might the more speedily come up. But they delayed in vain. At last a party went back in quest of the young lady, for Mrs. Hardy was naturally becoming apprehensive of her welfare. They proceeded on the route recently traversed, eagerly straining their eyes to catch some glimpses of the winsome form of the braw lassie; but they were unable to pierce the gloom which enveloped her fate. They shouted her name, but received in response only the sad echo of that sweetest of woman's titles. From glen and mountain-top—from crag and cliff—from rock and stream—"Mary" floated back to them on the wandering winds—a maddening, mocking echo.

Suddenly one of the men peers over a steep, shelving bank, and there, far below, beyond the power of human arm to reach or human foot to venture, he descries some articles of female apparel. Dobson at once recognizes the blue hood and the light grey mantle which Mary had worn.

Then the terrible truth flashes on them all. She has incautiously stepped on an insecure stone, and been hurled to swift destruction in the dismal and unfathomable abyss. And there, to confirm all of their horrid surmises, was the evidence of the earth having given way. What anguish then filled that bold man's heart. How his knees knocked together. How his face blanched. How he trembled and quivered as if smitten with sudden ague. He uttered no word of grief. His heart only beat with the violence of emotions that needed no voice. It clamored with beatings and throbbings and knockings, as if it would burst from its fleshly thrall, and leap out from its prison walls.

To break the intelligence to his wife taxed Dobson's strength. He could only utter those bitter words: "Lost, lost," and then gasp for breath, and burst out in great sobs. It was after a long continued effort that he succeeded in telling the whole story to the good woman–who listened to the melancholy tidings with downcast eyes, from which the tears ran in floods—all the while nervously twitching her dress, and constantly ejaculating an humble petition for mercy. When all had been told her, she cleared her voice, dashed her hand across her eyes, and said:

"God has kindly taken her home, where her mother is. It is right. She, too, might have been a sufferer from man's cruelty. God doeth all things well."

This revelation of the fact, that Mary was not the child of the Hardys, struck all those gathered about the camp-fire with great surprise. Her name, her tenderness and affectionate obedience—their unvarying kindness—a hundred little things had made all believe that the relationship between these persons was of the dearest and nearest and fondest character. Indeed, the bright girl sixteen years old, as she was, knew no better. She had always been accustomed to calling those good people father and mother. They were to her all that holy tie imports, and she had been living in blessed ignorance of her own parentage, so had all the world—these two people and the real parents alone excepted—until this sudden shock rent the veil which had hitherto enveloped her birth and ancestry.

X.

REDSTONE.

THIS terrible calamity cast a gloom over the entire company of emigrants, which the nearness of the end of their land journey, and the increasing beauty of the weather, could not remove. From their inner circle the bright particular star had been torn, and there were none but felt the loss as of a personal character. To all, Mary had endeared herself, by the remarkable amiability and sweetness of her disposition. She had a kind word and a bright smile for every one—the old and the young—master and slave. Did a baby cry, she would gladly relieve its care-worn mother. Did a little urchin fall or stub his toe, she would bind up the bruises and kiss away the tears. At night and on the Sabbath, she would read aloud from the Book of books to the admiring and wondering negroes, who would pronounce her readings as good as any "sermont;" and, indeed, it was a genuine pleasure to listen to the clear, delicious, and critically correct voice of the "young missus." Good reason, then, for mourning. They all knew that amid the trials of their new home, they would miss her cunning genius and her helping hand.

But our business is not that of eulogist, admirable as is the character under contemplation.

Late in the evening of the twelfth day after leaving Fort Cumberland, the guide, who was jogging along in advance, turned in his saddle-seat and cried: "The River!" In an instant the party was thrown into the utmost tumult. Never was cry heard and repeated with more enthusiasm,—not even when the van of the Ten Thousand Greeks, under Xenophon, first caught a glimpse of the blue Ægean, and shouted, "*θαλασσα, θαλασσα*," nor when Balboa looked out upon the Pacific's world of waters and claimed them for his sovereign.

All were eager to see the stream of which they had heard so much, and upon whose smooth current they were to float hundreds of miles. With questioning eyes they followed the direction the guide pointed, and through the thick trees saw a flash of water. Yes, there ran the Monongahela—narrow, deep, and swollen by the spring rains and the snow melting in the mountains. It was not very attractive in appearance just then, but they hailed it with every manifestation of delight. The road from the hill-top to the river bottom was winding and dangerous, so that they had to pick their way with care, and it was quite dark when they entered the aspiring village of Redstone—then the chief point of embarkation for western travellers.

And there, snugly ensconced about their last camp-fire, eating grilled venison and drinking mulled cider,—talking, and laughing, and singing, and whistling, using tongues, and arms, and teeth, and legs,—the half-sad, half-joyous company fought their battles over again, recounting their various haps and mishaps; but omitting any mention of the day when the terrible catastrophe occurred which so smote all hearts, and the ineffaceable remembrance of which causes yonder man and wife to sit apart, communing with their own voiceless woe.

XI.

AN ARK.

"HEW, hew! It's nuzzing but hew all ze day long. Rip, you minds me of ze Latin play—ze Thyestes of Ovid, vare all ze sad exclamations commence 'heu, heu!'"

"May I presume to correct your authority, sir? It was not Ovid who wrote that masterly tragedy, which, in the opinion of the great critic Quintilian, might bear comparison with the most perfect performance of the Greeks. Sir, it was Varius, a contemporary and friend of Virgil and Horace, who was an heir of the former, and appointed by Augustus to the task of revising the Æneid. But they do not read his pure Latin in these degenerate days. Hence, sir, doubtless your ignorance of his name."

This somewhat pompously pedantic speech

fell from the lips of Campbell, he having accidentally heard the remark which a volatile little Frenchman had addressed to a stalwart fellow who was hewing with his broad-axe, might and main, at a sweep-pole.

"Thank you, sare. May I have ze deep zatisfaction to know what scholar from ze University I meets here in ze wild wood? It is one long time since I hear a voice speak of ze Greek and ze Latin. *Bon ami*, give us your fist, as zey say out here."

"Oh, fiddle-sticks!" roars out the tall, raw-boned Rip, laying aside his bright keen axe. "Pooh, pooh! Little Frenchy, bear a hand here and stop your chaffing. We've got to stir our stumps; for if we don't, there'll be a fuss kicked up. Now, put your shoulder to the wheel and tug away at this oar. Let's make hay while the sun shines, and don't suffer the grass to grow under our feet. We're the boys to be up and stirring,—busy as bees, or a hen with one chicken."

While this sententious exhortation was being rolled out, the two were heaving away at the broad sweep, which was designed as part of the tackle of an ark lying in the river near them.

An Ark! First of marine craft. The safe bearer of Noah upon the wide world of waters. Hallowed by sacred recollections, and endeared by its agency in promoting the growth of the West. As from Adam all men came, so from the Ark has descended the long list of shipping from all ages and all countries—the fleets, navies, flotillas squadrons, and armadas—the line-of-battle-ship, the frigate, the sloop-of-war, the fire-ship, the transport, the bomb-vessel, the store-ship, and the tender. Yea, all the brigs, barks, brigantines, schooners, cutters, corvettes, clippers, skiffs, yawls, smacks, luggers, barges, lighters, steamers, steamboats, and steam-tugs. The whalers, coasters, slavers, colliers, long-boats, yachts, pinnaces, launches, shallops, jolly-boats, wherries, cock-boats, fishing-boats, life-boats, gondolas, feluccas, canoes, floats, rafts, galleys, galleons, galliots, and Chinese junks!

Truly, a very considerable array of descendants.

The morning after the arrival of our emigrants, they immediately commenced making arrangements for the river voyage. At least half a dozen arks would be required for the comfortable transportation of the familes, "plunder," and stock, and this number was speedily secured, for the tide of spring emigration had not yet set in, and the boat-builders had still on hand the fruits of their winter labors. It was also necessary to secure competent pilots; and hearing that the Indians were troublesome along the banks, the pioneers determined not to separate, but to combine their strength, so that the savages would be overawed by their formidable numbers.

Dobson Hardy was in search of a man to navi gate his boat, when he luckily fell in with Rip, who has already been introduced. Rip had been engaged for several years in piloting boats from Redstone to Limestone, and even, on one trip, had gone as far as the mouth of the Bear Grass. He was the very man for the place, if his own statements were received as true.

According to his account, he was "a regular rip snorter, a perfect fire-ball, battery, and siege-train; more frightensome to the Injuns than a Congreve rocket"—adding, by way of precaution, that he knew how to steer clear and fight shy of the bloody-minded rapscallions, and as for his prudence, you couldn't catch that weasel asleep—he always kept a sharp look-out, and had his eyes about him while he picked his own steps.

There was a heartiness of tone and manner about the bluff fellow which pleased Hardy, and he secured his services, employing as an assistant the little Frenchman, between whom and Rip there ad grown up the past winter a friendship as strong as it was unaccountable. Indeed, the boatman averred that his new-made friend was as giddy as a goose and mad as a March hare, talking like one possessed, and acting as if there were rats in his upper story.

XII.

AFLOAT.

IT was now Spring in reality. Well apparelled April had a week before made her appearance with fresh garb and elastic step and genial smile. Tripping over the lea, she had left flowers by banks and braes; had spread an emerald sheen over the brown, bare earth; had invoked the songs of birds; had aroused the lethargic frog to his croaking life; had tinged the sky with a deeper blue; had perfumed the air, crowned the woods, and made nature wear again her gala attire.

The river bore upon its cool, glassy, translucent wave, the flotilla of arks. Foremost of all was the boat of Hardy, with the redoubtable Rip at the helm. Following in close proximity were the other five; the decks of all lumbered with movables, while from the narrow windows at the sides there peered the visage of some astonished cow or startled horse. On board there was but a narrow division line between the possessions of quadrupeds and bipeds. The former occupied the bow, and the latter the stern, where a small cabin was arranged. Here, whites and blacks, children and man and wife were all huddled at night. Here they slept and cooked and ate. After sunset the occupants of the various boats would exchange visits, and seated upon the deck would listen to wild stories of western life—in narrating which the pilots were adepts—or join in a merry Virginia reel, keeping time to the music of the fiddle and banjo.

Thus the days and nights glided by; their flight scarcely heeded by the voyagers, who had resigned themselves to the gentle current, and were content that it should bear them along on its own placid bosom, according to its own sweet will.

At Fort Pitt the Alleghany and Monongahela rivers unite, forming the Ohio. The day that the arks floated into the widened stream the wind freshened up from the south, and the water was agitated in miniature waves. The boats were tossed about by the restless water,

XIII.

HOW THE RIVER OHIO OBTAINED ITS NAME.

THE idea prevailed for some time that the word Ohio was derived from the Iroquois language, the Indians of that tribe calling it the fine and beautiful, and, sometimes, the bloody river. But in the vocabularies of that language there are no words corresponding with these terms. The better hypothesis is, that Ohio is derived from the Delawares, and signifies white, or the white foaming river. Ohio, however, is not the whole Indian name. It has evidently been considerably abbreviated by the French and English, who, as is their custom, always drop a portion of every aboriginal word, in order to render the pronunciation easy.

Among the words which have gone to form the name of the river are the following, from the Delaware:

O'hui—ohi, very.

O'peu, white.

Opelecheu, bright, shining.

Opeek, white with froth.

Ohio-pecheu, it is of a white color.

Ohio-peek, very white, caused by froth or white caps.

Ohio-phaune, very white stream.

Ohio-peek-haune, very deep and white stream, by its being covered over with white caps.

Ohio-peh-hele, white frothy water.

As you have observed, this river being in many places wide and deep, and so gentle that there is scarcely any perceptible current, the least wind blowing up-stream covers the surface with white caps, rendering the navigation in canoes difficult and dangerous. Hence the Indians, when the river was covered with these white foaming swells, would say: "Juh Ohio-pecheu," and when it was very deep: "Kitchi Ohio-peek-haune"—verily, this is a deep, white river.

How the word Ohio came to be so universally used in designating the river is easily inferred. The early emigrants very naturally took the first syllable of the Indian name "Ohio-peek-haune," since it could be pronounced without difficulty, and readily retained in the memory.

From this theory, which may be received or rejected at the option of the reader, the Frenchman elaborated an hour's discourse full of learning, which would be more appropriate in the transactions of the American Antiquarian Society, than here among pages designed to relieve the tedium of idle hours.

XIV.

A DECOY.

IN this apparently careless manner the arks floated down the stream, but as they approached the mouth of the Kanawha the vigilance of the pilot, which had not been even for a moment relaxed, was doubled. They were now entering into a dangerous region. The river scenery had increased in beauty. The hills were greener—the level bottoms clad in ranker and riper vegetation—the beach on either shore was pebbly and smooth, and the white and particolored sand glistened in the sunlight. It did not seem possible that scenes so fair as these through which they passed could be marred by demoniac passions of men. There was that in the calm, quiet and unbroken repose of nature which seemed to forbid aught but the exercise of the gentler attributes of humanity. Yet the life-blood of hundreds had crimsoned this crystal stream. These forests had echoed the savage yell of fury, and the listening oaks had shuddered at the cry of helpless agony from the lips of tortured pale-faces. The sky, now so bright, had been darkened with the clouds from the burning stake where prisoners were offered up as holocausts to the fiend spirit, and the very air had been heavy with sighs and sobs and execrations.

Fortunately the river was high and no danger was to be apprehended from shoals, sand-bars or sawyers. These obstructions to navigation were hidden from sight, and there was no difficulty in ascertaining the proper channel, for it embraced the whole stream.

The night scenes on board had been materially changed. Now the utmost silence was enjoined. Not one word was to be whispered, except from necessity, and then with bated breath. They knew not at what point a band of Indians might be lurking, and their aim was to steal quietly by under the protecting shade of darkness, without attracting notice and attack. Each evening the sweeps were unshipped, and the muffled steering-pole was alone used. This was done to increase the stillness. Besides, these rude boatmen understood a law of physics which rendered them the more willing to rest on their oars after sunset. This law is, that a boat will float faster at night than in the day—in fact will float alone and unaided at night as fast as by the aid of both oars and current in the day-time. The same principle enables a miller to grind more in an equal period between sunset and sunrise than sunrise and sunset, and a saw-mill to cut a greater amount of lumber by night than by day—water-mills, of course.

The whys and wherefores of these facts we do not care to explain, philosophy not being our forte. However, they can be accounted for very reasonably on the ground of the increased specific gravity of water at night; as well as ascribed to the vapors which being held in suspension in the upper regions of the air by day, descend at night and by their weight and density increase the momentum of the water.

They had proceeded thus cautiously for some time without discovering any Indian signs, and Rip, though no coward and rather fond of a scrimmage, was congratulating himself on hav-escaped an attack. But just then his complacency of manner was considerably disturbed. The sharp crack of a rifle awoke the echoes, and repeating itself through the neighboring hills, there seemed to have been a volley fired. His boat still maintained the lead. Turning to observe the cause of this unusual occurrence, he saw instantly, as he remarked, "a storm was brewing, and the devil was to pay." Just at the bend in the rear was the last boat floating leisurely along, no man at the helm and none at the sweeps. The people were crowded at one side, eagerly gazing toward the shore, and thither the hawk-eyed Rip directed his observation. A skiff was just striking the bank, from which two men leaped. The first was our Scottish friend Campbell, with his long rifle, and the other the pilot of the laggard boat. Their feet had scarcely made an impression on the yielding sand before bang, bang went other rifles—wreaths of light-blue smoke discovering the ambuscade of a party of Indians. Palsied by the attack from unseen foes, the two men stood immovable, their rifles raised to their shoulders and pointed at the thin and unsubstantial air. While standing thus statue-like they were grasped from behind, and their arms would have been pinioned had not Campbell turned upon his heel with such swiftness and force that the outstretched barrel of his gun felled one of the Indians. It was but the work of a second to discharge its contents at the other, whc fell prostrate, his skull pierced by a bullet. The red-skin who lay senseless on the sand from the effects of the blow, was then dispatched. So much that was unexpected being thus accomplished in so short a time, the two men wisely thought that discretion would be the better part of valor, pushed their skiff from the beach and were soon skimming the water.

This conflict had been observed with emotions of alarm and apprehension from all the boats, and they were now moored close together, in order to act more securely and compactly on the defensive, should there be a further attack, which seemed altogether probable.

The raw-boned Scot, who had just tasted his first blood, and was yet tremulous with the effects of the sharp contest, was lifted on board Rip's boat. That worthy, who by common consent was acknowledged admiral of the fleet, received him very heartily, if somewhat brusquely.

"Well done, you long-armed, awkward gaited loon! them's the licks to put in when you'd save your own scalp-knot. But whar's the Injuns' scalps? Bless me if the fellers warn't in too big a hurry to take the head-dress of the screamin' red savages. Why that battle warn't half won."

"Yea, sir," answered Campbell, who had somewhat regained his composnre, and whose face, so flushed and heated and passionate from the emotions of the conflict, was rapidly resuming its wonted aspect of grave stolidity. "Yea, but I needs be in a hurry. How did I know but that the woods might be full of savages? Moreover, it was only necessity that made me slay the two Indians. I had no desire to mangle them afterward."

"Too tender and chicken-hearted was you. Well, I never seed the time when I wouldn't have butchered and mommicked and slaughtered the cantankerous devils. Why, man, with them two scalps dangling at your belt you might have made your fortin among the gals when you go a galivantin' about the station whar you intend squattin'. Nothin' like glory for the feminines. They hitch right off to a feller who has smelt powder. But what on airth did you go ashore fur? Now you've raised the whole country, and sich a caterwaulin' as we'll have 'fore midnight!"

"Well, sir, since you demand what we went ashore for, let me say that we were prompted by the highest and loftiest dictates of benevolence. We went, sir, to render assistance to a poor woman of our own Caucasian complexion, who was piteously beckoning for assistance, and who was about being attacked by a huge and rampant wild beast."

This statement of the Caledonian Campbell was received by Rip with a loud laugh.

"Fooled, by hoky!—And you," turning to the pilot who had been a partner in the excursion, "had you no more gumption. Oh, you beetle-headed, beef-witted spoonies! you blunder-headed, clod-pated, dull-brained, dim-sighted jabber-nowls! You are regular ninny-hammers! I reckon you won't go on sich a wild goose chase soon again."

Campbell listened patiently to these objurgations of Rip, uncertain how to regard his extravaganzas of diction; while Jake, the pilot, slunk away in the crowd, heartily ashamed of having been caught napping.

"What become of your woman and the bar?

Hain't you got sense enough to see it was a reg'lar trick? The cunnin' devils jest set her thar to make pretence, and then one of the rascals throwed a bar skin over him to make believe he was after the woman. But they can't ketch this here Rip Snorter with any sich contrivances. I'm up to snuff, wide awake and full of fleas. But you're a sojer, Scotch friend, and kin shoot. We're likely to have warm work afore long, and you must be ready to draw a bead on 'em to some 'vantage. Now let's all to our own crafts. Put the wimmen and children and nigs belows decks; let one man tend the steerin' oar; pile up the plunder, so there'll be a kind of barricade, and then lay low and keep dark. But see, yonder's that witch which liked to prove the death of Jake and Campbell. Shall I give her a taste of my dare-all? It's a long while since the old dog has barked at anything human."

Some one interposed an objection, and the boatman replied;

"Well. I reckon it wouldn't do to shoot a woman, even if she does lay traps and snares. That's her nature. They are always trying to fool us chaps, somehow."

Sure enough, there, more than a mile from the scene of the recent encounter, stood a lone female figure. She waved her hands and arms with frantic gesticulations, but no words escaped her lips. Occasionally she would glance about her as if fearful of discovery, and then renew her silent appeals for succor. The voyagers were too wary now to be decoyed by this semblance of destitution and desertion, and heedless of the exciting pantomime on the bank, proceeded on the noiseless tenor of their way.

Presently a splash in the water strikes their sharp ears, and looking shoreward they see the woman struggling in the stream. She strikes out boldly toward the boats, her black, dishevelled hair floating behind her, and her gaunt, woe-begone face, just above the surface of the water, looks as if misery and despair had been stamped on every feature. While she is thus energetically battling with the tide, a party of Indians appear on the bank, and levelling their guns, ball after ball strikes the water near where the poor woman is buffeting the waves. One bullet cuts a tress of her hair, and soon after a jet of dark blood spurts up on the green water.

This was too much for Campbell to witness unmoved. Forgetting the danger he had so recently escaped, and caring now for no one to share his adventures, he again leaps into the little skiff, and rows to the assistance of the distressed woman. His aid was timely, for exhausted by her struggles, she was about sinking, when the daring Scot snatched her from a yawning grave. He did not perform this rescue without jeopardy. The savages, safe behind the trees, no sooner saw his efforts than they blazed away at him. It fairly rained bullets, but none struck them; although the leaden messengers sung and whistled about their ears fiercely and furiously. The skiff was not so fortunate. Its sides were soon perfectly riddled, and in a few moments Campbell found it rapidly filling with water. Thus he was again placed in an awkward predicament; but unused as he was to such emergencies, he did not give up. There was a fertility of expediency about him which is common to people of sluggish impulses, and which rarely, if ever, fails of proving effective in the hour of the utmost need. Placing his rifle between his teeth, and clasping the fainting woman with his left arm, he struck out with the right, and had reached his boat before his astonished comrades could go to his assistance.

Safe on board, although most thoroughly drenched, and nearly fagged out by his exertions, Campbell would not leave his protégée whom he had so valiantly rescued. He even denied the females the privilege of assisting in the work of restoring her to consciousness. With a tenderness of manner that seemed misplaced in one so rude and outré in general deportment, the Scot chafed her limbs and smoothed her shining hair, and applied a drop of pure brandy to her tongue, and pressed his face close beside hers, but not to kiss those pallid lips. Only to see if the slightest breath of life escaped. His exertions were at last crowned with success. The eyes opened wildly—the breast heaved as if it would throw off the accumulation of years of sorrow, and then subsided into a calm and regular swell, as if peace was once more enthroned there. She was yet too much enfeebled to speak. Pointing to her bare shoulder, she gave Campbell a look of ineffable gratitude—a thank offering from the heart for his attention—and then relapsed into a state of semi-consciousness.

By this time Rip, whose curiosity had been

highly excited by the incident just narrated, and who had awaited patiently on his boat to have a report presented, as he presumed would be done, in deference to his seniority, jumped into his skiff and paddled over to investigate what he regarded "a very queer proceedin'."

He found Campbell kneeling beside the woman, busily engaged in bandaging the wound, over which he had spread a poultice of "sweet yarbs," speedily prepared by one of the female voyagers. Having finished his work, he turned to see who had stepped so heavily, and was greeted by Rip, who shook his hand cordially, and praised him as a bold fellow, though he would run needless risks.

"But, as for my part," continued Rip, "I'm in favor of a headlong, dare-devil man like you, who goes post-haste, head foremost on a forlorn hope. It's a kind of temptin' Providence that I think Providence don't much object to."

Campbell, who was as modest as he had just discovered himself to be intrepid, begged his friend to withhold any applause. "I only desired the commendation of my own conscience, and that I have," said he, with an eloquent gesture toward his heart.

"Well, Scotchy," replied Rip, "I'll hold up; but I knowed praise wouldn't spile you, nor make you give yourself airs. You ain't of the sort that are so easily perked up."

The two then engaged in conversation, Campbell all the while watching with tender solicitude the deep, untroubled breathing of the fragile waif cast into his arms by the river. With a smile that shed a halo about her dark face, she slowly opened her eyes, and seeing that she was safe among friends, only ejaculated, "Thank God!" It was several minutes before she spoke again, and then, not until she had cast a penetrating, searching glance toward the thickly wooded shore.

"They intend attacking you to-night. There are two hundred warriors painted and dressed for the war-dance, and they want scalps. Not far below this, upon a point of land that projects far out into the river, and where the trees from either side almost lap and form an arch, they have made their camp. There the women are cooking the feast, and they only wait your coming to revel in your blood, and whet their appetites with murder and violence before they sit down to the banquet. Men, you must save yourselves, as you can, if you are all heroes like this good man who snatched me from death. But you must be cool and calm, and keep well together."

"That, good woman, is what I've been tryin' to cram into 'em, and I think we'll make a purty good fight, be they two hundred or two thousand of the whoopin', screechin', murderin', rapin red devils."

Night had now fully descended. The river gleamed with the reflection of myriads of stars. Only the low, sullen plash of the water against the gunwales of the boats, was to be heard. A degree of silence that could almost be felt, hovered about the little company. From the shores came no sound; not even the cheerful chirp of a cricket; not the hoarse croak of a frog; not the voice of the katy-did; not even the musical murmur of the leafy trees.

Through the awful gloom and solemn hush of the night—with almost certain death before them, and no refuge behind, toward which they could turn—between forests peopled with deadly foes, and over the glassy bosom of the river whose treacherous embrace would stifle all hope and life, the voyagers floated on. But the cold iron of despair had not yet entered their souls, The diamond stars and the cloudless sky, so clear and purely beautiful, assured them "That God alone was to be seen in Heaven."

XV.

THE BATTLE NIGHT.

AS they had been forewarned by the strange woman, the monotony of this hushed and death-like silence was soon broken. Turning a curve of the river, light after light flashed upon them through the trees and undergrowth. For a quarter of a mile along the northern bank there were blazing log fires, about which, in the wild delirium of savage joy, the Indians danced. Pandemonium itself seemed to have been turned loose. The savages accompanied their weird and frenzied exercises with every conceivable description of noise. Confusion was indeed worse confounded in this scene. They gave voice to their own instincts, and imitated every beast of the field and fowl of the air. They roared, shouted, bawled, whooped, yelled, hooted, howled, screamed, screeched, shrieked, squeaked, squalled, whined, piped, moaned, groaned, snorted, barked, yelped, growled, neighed, brayed, croaked, snarled, mewed, bleated, cawed, cackled, gobbled, and quacked.

To use the expressive, though somewhat profane phrase of Rip, "it was a perfect hellaballoo."

The watch-fires threw out broad sheets of baleful light quite across the river, so that the boats in vain hugged the left bank, hoping thereby to escape detection. That, indeed, would have been an impossibility, for they soon discovered that the wary savages, determined not to allow them to escape, had stretched across the stream a cordon of boats filled with wild and fantastically dressed warriors. The six arks, lashed together, swept on with the force of the current, and were almost immediately upon the warrior-laden skiffs. Such was the impetus, that they crushed down several of these frail barks, and a score of Indians were soon struggling in the water. Volley after volley was discharged, but not a white could be seen. The fleet was silent as the grave, and seemed guided by an invisible hand. Nor was the fire of the savages returned. Still, they continued to pour out their death-dealing missiles, until, mystified and alarmed by the ominous silence, they prepared to board. The first Indian who leaped on the ark was instantly felled by an axe, wielded by some unseen power. Others followed, but shared the same fate, and fell into the bright water, which closed over them with a gurgle, half melancholy and half joyful.

This was on Hardy's boat, which had been placed foremost as a bulwark, being the strongest. Defending it, were Hardy, Rip, the little Frenchman, with Tom and Cash, the two negro men. That they made a stout resistance the death of more than a score of the enemy was testimony sufficient. But, valiant and active as they were, they could not resist the overwhelming odds. After a fierce hand to hand conflict—in which the little Frenchman, who was dealing his blows right and left with a gory axe, was cut down—they were forced back upon one of the other boats. At this juncture, the Hardy boat was cut loose, and drifted away with its deck crowded by the rioting savages.

So desperate and general had the contest become, that no one noticed the drifting boat, save the strange woman. She knew that the wife and children were aboard, as well as the stock and valuables of the family. Determined that these should not be irretrievably lost without one effort being made for their salvation, she cut loose a skiff, and, gliding noiselessly away from the battle boats, moored alongside the Hardy ark. She quietly opened the rear window, and, with a "hist" to prevent alarm, bade Mrs. Hardy prepare for an escape. This was not an easy undertaking, but she succeeded in pulling the mother and children through the small aperture. It was more difficult to release Aunt Milly, the old negro, but she was finally drawn through—her immense rotundity of flesh and all. In this labor, the heroic rescuer was not disturbed by the Indians on deck, for they had found a keg of liquor, and were swilling it, oblivious of all things else. Just as the heavily laden skiff was pushing off, they heard a low groan from the interior of the boat, and Mrs. Hardy then remembered that the little Frenchman, after being wounded, had fallen down the hatch and was lying on the floor. It was impossible at that time to afford him any succor. So the woman rowed away to one of the rearmost boats, where she safely deposited her cargo. She then pursued the floating ark, solicitous of recovering the wounded man. Tying her boat on the side where the deep shadows lay, she reëntered, and groping her way in the dark she soon stumbled over a prostrate body. The poor fellow was too weak from loss of blood to offer any resistance, and was dragged out by the noble woman, to whom courage and danger had seemingly imparted herculean strength. Anxious, not only to rescue these unfortunate people, but to wreak her vengeance upon the dastardly red ruffians, she had prepared a bundle of light wood, and before taking a final leave of the boat, placed it in a central position near the stores, and where, she hoped, the magazine of powder was kept. Lighting the wood, she hurriedly left and took her place in the skiff. She had not progressed a dozen yards when there was a loud report—the air was filled with blazing fragments, and timbers, and the mutilated bodies of Indians. In the darkness of the night the meteoric splendor of the explosion revealed the skiff tossing upon the agitated waters, the dark face of the lone woman gloating with joy over the ruin she had accomplished, while the poor Frenchman, just able to cling to his seat, gazed with a ghastly smile upon the wreck, unconscious of where he was, or how surrounded.

Meanwhile, the battle had been raging. It was an unequal contest in regard to numbers; but to the whites, who were contending for life, God gave the victory. The terrific explosion of the floating ark struck terror into the hearts of the savages, who had already been daunted by the stubborn resistance of the pale-faces. Then another occurrence added to their consternation. Suddenly the sky was overcast:

> "Ipse pater, media nimborum in nocte, corusca
> Fulmina molitur dextra."

Confused, stunned, and alarmed at these elementary disturbances, the Indians gave way. Instantly the whites were animated with fresh courage, and with clubbed guns and sharp axes they drove the foe overboard. But it was some time before they could realize the actuality of their safety, and the morning was glimmering in the east when they gathered together to return thanks for their wonderful deliverance.

XVI.

THE LOST FOUND.

NATURE delights in contrasts, and employs her skillful magic in rendering them as effective and startling as possible. The morning after the battle and storm, was as beautiful and placid as a cherub's slumber. Every tree and leaf and shrub glistened with renewed beauty and freshness. The river had resumed its gentleness, and lay about them like a vast mirror, in which the fleecy cloudlets were reflected, and the overhanging sycamores were imaged with perfect trace and lineament. The air was odorous with the freightage of the sweet South, which had been loitering and dallying amid the glorious luxuriance of the Canetuckey forests. From either shore came the liquid minstrelsy of rival choristers. There was a gladness and a rapture in the sounds of earth and sky that almost effaced the memories of the terrific night encounter.

Apart from the others sat Mrs. Hardy and the woman whose mysterious appearance and whose unexampled heroism we have already detailed. Gratitude prompted Mrs. H. to seek out her deliverer, and thank her, as she had thanked the God of both, for the fortunate and daring rescue. But she refused to listen to words of praise, and mute, she would neither talk nor desire to be talked to. Our Fauquier dame, however, was of a persevering character, and she plied her questions so incessantly, and yet with such delicacy, that the stranger felt the ice of restraint gradually melting about her heart, and she was soon in a full flood of confidential disclosure.

No one disturbed them as they communed through the bright morning hours. The decks, slippery with blood, were to be cleansed. The three cold, clammy corpses were to be prepared for burial. The wounded were to be ministered to—there was employment for all.

But why are tears standing in the eyes of Mrs. Hardy? Why does sob after sob burst from her lips? Why does her breast heave tumultuously? Why does she throw her arms about this strange woman and clasp her home to her own bosom? Strange woman no longer. Those hours of quiet, earnest, subdued conversation have resulted in a revelation as startling as it is joyful. Through the tangled meshes of the dialogues we need not drag the reader. The result arrived at is, that Mrs. Hardy has discovered her twin sister—the wife of the perfidious Burkitt—a sister long supposed to be dead, now found, and rescued from a living grave!

The story is a long one, but we can condense it after the fashion of the newspaper paragraphists. As those classical, erudite and accomplished wielders of pen, paste and scissors say, we shall give *multum in parvo*. Or, to borrow the language of Rip Snorter, Esq., here is the truth in a nut-shell.

Through all the campaigns of the war of Independence, Mrs. Burkitt had followed the fortunes of her husband. Her lot had been a grievous one—full of wretchedness and want and degradation, crowned by cruelty and neglect from her sworn defender, to whom she had adhered with wifely tenacity, excusing his outrages on law and order, forgiving his brutalities to her, and living day by day with a trembling hope that God would smite the heart of the wicked man with a sense of his evil doing. But her hopes were deferred, and her heart grew sick. Burkitt plunged into a deeper vortex of sin and crime, and seemed ambitious of finding a still lower deep in the deepest depths of which he could revel a devil-possessed miscreant. Occasionally some gleams of his better nature would shine forth. These, falling upon the bruised heart of the poor wife, warmed into new life affections and trustfulness that might else have faded away forever. At the close of the Revolutionary struggle, knowing that it would be impossible to remain in the colonies, they had fled through the wilderness to the line of British posts. Subsequently, Burkitt had joined the Indians, becoming that most hated and detested of all characters—a renegade white. He had been for a year past foremost in all marauding expeditions against the whites, and was only satisfied when engaged in some scheme of pillage and murder. About New Year's he left the Indian village on Paint River, and since then had not been heard from. Supposing, from his protracted absence, that the avenging Nemesis had at last overtaken him in his career of crime, she determined to make an effort for her restoration to civilized life. Fortunately the Indians favored her plan, although unintentionally on their part. The day before, having ascertained that a number of arks were descending the river, they compelled her to go up with a small party of warriors, and act as a decoy—pretending to be in distress, and seeking relief. She had thus been thrown into the arms of her sister.

This is the story in brief. We did not dare attempt giving it in the language—simple, forcible, and at times picturesquely eloquent—of the reciter. We might as well have aimed at portraying, in our feeble words, the varying shadows of her face, the bursts of passionate grief, the starts and alarms which the recall of passages in her experience excited.

Wisely Mrs. Hardy withheld from her sister any account of her own knowledge of Burkitt's recent career. She knew that the shame and ignominy to which he had been subjected, and of which she was an involuntary witness, would only add to the bitterness of her grief.

But of her child—that brown-haired girl who had been intrusted to her guardianship when in its puling infancy—she did not see it here—what of it? Had her fortune been love and honorable marriage, or shame and miserable death? Tell her. She could bear anything.

Accordingly, Mrs. Hardy, in her calm, cold voice, now and then choked with emotion, told her bereaved sister of the glad, bright girl just blossoming into womanhood, who had been so mysteriously, so causelessly (as it appeared to human eyes) removed.

"God doeth all things well," was the mother's reply—the very same words that Mrs. Hardy had used when first informed of the loss of Mary.

Comforting text! Balm to grieved spirits, assuaging the wounds and healing the bruises of crushed and lacerated hearts! How rich is the divine word in such blessed assurances of the divine care and love!

XVII.

LANDING AT LIMESTONE.

"HERE'S the Three Islands, and it's thirteen miles to Limestone. The sun is yet more than an hour high, and if we will pull altogether we can reach a harbor of safety before nightfall."

This promise of Rip's endowed the wearied and overworked boatmen with new energy. They shuddered at the prospect of spending another night upon the river. Already their fancies were peopling the woods with enemies, and the air seemed voiceful with the savage cries and noises that had saluted them the night before. Their vexed and tried brains were in fit condition for freaks of the imagination.

With a lively yo-ho, they manned the sweeps and sped along at an astonishing rate. At every bend in the river they looked forward anxiously to see if there was yet any sign of the long hoped for Limestone. Down behind the leaf-crowned hills, his broad disc clear and brilliant, attended by an argosy of golden, rose, pink, purple and saffron cloud-ships, the sun had gone, and the twilight of a spring evening was mantling the face and form of nature.

At last, through the thickening shadows, they descry the long sought haven.

The noise of their busily plied oars and the rowing chorus, in which they all unite with glad heartiness, arouse the dwellers in the cabins on the shore, and as they move into the sheltered harbor, formed by the creek which debouches into the river, a crowd of men, women and children gather on the bank to welcome these new-comers—aye, to welcome them to the toils and tribulations and rewards of pioneer life.

In that group, standing with arms akimbo, and rifle leisurely resting against his shoulder, six feet two in his moccasined feet, erect as a pine and handsome as Apollo, is one figure to be remarked at any time and in any place as not of the common mold and build.

In those old times—gone now these five and seventy years—Limestone was a village of three log huts. Ned Waller was the *genius loci*, and for the ultimate grandeur of this, his chosen abode, he eloquently prophesied between drunken hiccoughs. Three quarters of a century work many changes in men and things, towns and people. Is it not true, as King Lothario I. said, according to that German-Latinist poet, Matthias Borbonius:

> "Tempora mutantur, nos et mutamur in illis."

The magnificence and glory and renown of which this Bacchanal prophet spoke, in his wavering accents, may have been vouchsafed Limestone. Of it we know nothing. We do know this, however, that time and the barbaric taste of man has despoiled that little bit of landscape of half the beauties wherewith nature had originally so lavishly endowed it.

The secluded cove in which the arks of our emigrants moored has given way to a rough stone wharf—the pleasant little stream flowing from the hills and through the valleys, and humming a quiet tune as it ebbed among the green alders and the tall flags and kissed the drooping willows and eddied around the huge sycamores —that glassy stream is only a memory now. A railway in ruins, rotten trestle-work, foul and fœtid slaughter-houses—these have destroyed the romance and marred the beauty of as sweet a piece of uncultivated nature as was ever dropped from the All-shaping Hand.

And that seven acre tract of woodland—then a miniature park, with its lofty trees and its velvet sward and its glimpses of water—has been ruthlessly destroyed to make room for what sober people seriously style a city! *Vanitas vanitatum!*

"As I live, if here arn't Simon Kenton," exclaimed Hardy, when the athletic, iron-framed and classically featured pioneer, clad in his hunting shirt, buckskin leggins and bearskin hat, appeared on the ark to greet the emigrants.

Astonished to hear his name so familiarly pronounced in that far region, where it had been until then unsyllabled, the stalwart hunter drew up his lofty form, and with a questioning glance took in, at one sweep of his eagle eye, the entire proportions of Hardy.

"And when did you get into these latitudes? You were given up for lost long ago, and your father and mother have had your name written down in the Bible as dead. They wore mourning for you a year or more."

These latter allusions started a tear to the eye of Kenton, which, stoic of the woods as he was, he could not repress.

The other people of Limestone were not a little astonished by this interview. But why, we shall tell you by and by.

Kenton found in Hardy an old family friend, and was rejoiced that fate had thrown in his path one from whom he could ascertain definite intelligence concerning his long deserted home. Understanding that Hardy had lost boat, plunder, stock and all, save life and hope, by the Indian attack, with characteristic kindness he insisted upon his accompanying him home and making that his headquarters until he could enter a tract of land and build a cabin.

Hardy at any other time would have been reluctant to accept an offer of this nature, for dependence, even momentarily, was something his proud nature scorned. But this tender was made in the spirit of ancient friendship, and could not have been rejected without wounding the sensitiveness of a lofty heart. That the newly found sister and the wounded little Frenchman, who, we might as well now introduce as Pierre Savary, should likewise share the hospitalities of Kenton's station, was also agreed upon.

Thither we will accompany the party.

XVIII.

THE BREEZY HILL-TOP OF SUGAR LOAF.

STAND here awhile. Uncover, and allow the breath of May to kiss your forehead, to dally with your locks, to brighten your cheeks. It is fresh from the bosky dells, where the naiads and dryads hold their revels—where the anemone blossoms and the meek-eyed violet looks heavenward. Does it not bear the scent of rich earth? It has journeyed over those blossoming fields and through those dark-green woods; it has skimmed the surface of yonder shining river; it has wafted those white clouds to the far horizon. Freighted with health—joy-giving—a reveller in shady coverts and in the blue, untracked abysses of the upper deep—breeze of heaven's own inspiration, musical as it pipes through the quivering foliage, delicious as a draught of nectar—how it loves to loiter upon this hill-top.

It is a weary way up, and the path is stony and rough. There are briers to prick the struggler, and slippery places where the feet must be securely planted. But the brave heart and the stout limb never tire. It is the way of life—ever up-hill to the heights of bliss.

Look out now! Are you not recompensed for your toils by the green and glorious panorama spread at your feet? Note the lovely scene encircled by the amphitheatre of wooded hills. How long—for ages, during more years than there are stars on the breast-plate of heaven—they have lifted their tall heads up toward the everlasting hills where our God and fathers tread the *via sacra.* In winter, mantled with snow—in spring, wreathed with green—in summer, wearing the full crown of matured nature—in autumn, blazing with robes more brilliant than oriental sovereigns ever wore.

Miles far away, there gushes through a woody barrier—bright, broad, and beautiful in its strength—the Ohio. You can see it as it laves the sloping banks, glistening in the sun and darkening in the shadow. Like a belt of molten silver it lays athwart the landscape—eternal as the skies that arch over it and the hills which throw their shades upon its bosom.

Enchanted valleys, and gentle declivities, and tall precipices, and flashing waterfalls, and wild gorges, and wooded plains—with the brisk little city nestling among them all—these are the master-strokes of nature in the scenery, which you cannot fail admiring as you stand on the breezy hill-top of Sugar Loaf, overlooking Limestone!

XIX.

SIMON KENTON.

THIRTEEN years before the period of which we are now writing, Simon Kenton, then at the age of sixteen years, fell in love, and consequently, in trouble.

Ah! sixteen is a dangerous era in the life of youth who possess that imaginary function—a heart. No matter the sex—sweet sixteen, or rowdy sixteen—over all there steals the sentiment that fond fools call love and wise bachelors know is bosh! It affects Augustus Pipestemlegs in the city, and Simon Sturdyshanks in the woods. It gives a palpitation of the "buzzum" to Sophronisba Hoopdedoodledo in the Fifth Avenue, and Betsey Jane Skirtless in Iowa. Love, when the patient is a sixteen-year-old, is like the spring fever, very contagious; but it never affects the appetite, and convalescence soon follows. With old George Withers, a poet of the year of grace 1588, the lover, slighted by a girl in her first season of coquetry, whistles·

"Shall I, wasting in despair,
Dye because a woman's fair?
Or make pale my cheeks with care
'Cause another's rosie are?
If she be not so to me
What care I how fair she be?"

Kenton had a rival—one Veach—who was more successful than he. This rivalry led to blows and a certain encounter, in which Ken ton tied the long hair of his opponent to a young sapling, and then pummelled him until he supposed that he was dead. Revenge is sweet, especially when you can wreak it upon one who has stolen your sweetheart; but when Kenton saw the pale face and felt the pulseless arm, and could detect no sign of respiration, he would have given up all the girls in Fauquier and Culpepper could he but have felt one throb of his enemy's heart, and known that he still lived. Alarmed at his murderous deed, he fled, and for years lived the life of a refugee, under the name of Simon Butler, in the wild woods.

In the midst of his wanderings he heard of the unexampled fertility of this region, abounding in cane and turkey. Kenton always held that the title of the State was a corruption from the combined names of the two great staples—cane and wild turkeys. Caneturkey! What thinkest thou, O etymologist?"

Here he had planted the first corn ever raised north of the Kentucky River; here he had established his post in the very van of the pioneer army—within a rifle-shot of the Indian settlements. He had not seated himself in the far interior, two days' journey from the frontiers and the foe, but at the very threshold had thrown down the glove of defiance.

It was with utmost satisfaction that he heard Hardy relate the recovery of the nearly-murdered Veach. There existed no longer any reason for wearing an assumed name, and he resumed the appellation of his father with feelings of no little pride. Thenceforth he wore his own name, and wore it honorably through a half century of years, every one of which was crowded with trials sufficient to have crushed the spirit of an ordinary man.

But all these hardships of mature life were

only repetitions of his youthful grievances. His mind had received no cultivation whatever. Not the slightest knowledge of letters was imparted to him. In total ignorance of the most common rudiments of education, he grew up to manhood without a single gleam of learning illuminating and giving peace and pleasure to the hours of relaxation from toil.

Thus ignobly passed his childhood, with its guileless heart hardened by wrong—its sunny temper clouded by austerity—its buoyant spirits dejected by oppression—its winsome ways clogged by boorish associations.

Youth, with its hot blood and high aspirations, opened before him. But the future common to us all—to the hopeful vision, a fairy land of bright skies, flashing waters, laurel crowns, and golden happiness, was veiled from his sight by the clouds of poverty and neglect.

But despite all these obstacles, Kenton battled heroically, like the true hero that he was. With his blood he purchased the virgin forests and fields of northern Kentucky from savage possession. Generous, confiding, and unsuspecting by nature, these very excellences of his heart rendered him liable to fraud and imposition.

He located large tracts of land, and should have seen his old age blessed with affluence; but designing men, whom his liberality had enriched, impoverished him, and, like the old Romans, he and his sons were forced to leave the fields their valor had won.

> "Nos patriæ fines, et dulcia linquimus arva;
> Nos patriam fugimus."

Cast in jail, and deprived of his liberty for two years—not for crime, but poverty—at the instigation of the persons whose fortunes he had made, and who thus sadly requited his generosity, by cheating him out of his hard-earned property, the old hero found relief in flight to the wilds of northwestern Ohio, where he died peacefully in his cabin.

If to-day you ride along that magnificent thoroughfare, leading from the Ohio at Maysville toward Lexington, you will pass beside smiling fields and green pastures, palatial farmhouses, and handsome villages. There is no fairer land in our State—none where plenty, with her bright train, scatters gifts with such lavish hands. There orchards bloom, and the sweet clover is odorous through the spring-time.

There the golden grain waves in seas of yellow through the summer. There the green hemp flings its perfumes upon the air. The corn rustles, sleek cattle feed, and the coaches of rural Dives roll by and dash the dust in your face if you are but a common footpad.

And all these smiling woods and green fields were once Kenton's. But his ample possessions were torn from him by land pirates. The children of the men who swindled the veteran, who imposed upon his credulity, and took advantage of his child-like simplicity, now dwell in state upon the very lands his toils, and privations, and prowess won from pagan and barbaric possession.

XX.

WE DISCUSS WOMAN'S WEAKNESS.

"MADAME I see not how I can leave you; my heart it goes pit-a-pat to you. I could take you *à bras ouverts*. Oh! I will go down to you *à genoux*. But say you bear me one affection and I could die; but say you be mine and I shall live your humble valet. Do not think I am a vaurien—one good for nothing fellow."

Such was the interjectional love-making of Pierre to his kind nurse, Mrs. Burkitt. The little fellow, who had been most attentively cared for, and whose gun-shot wound had healed very rapidly, considering that there was no surgical assistance rendered—the more rapidly and surely perhaps from the lack of a surgeon—in the fullness of his gratitude, knew no other way of giving vent to his feelings than by this protestation of love. It is a characteristic French method—a demonstrative way that excitable and impetuous people have; not that they mean half they utter in these impetuous bursts. Thus it was with Pierre. His life had been saved by the daring intrepidity of Mrs. Burkitt. In his hours of pain she had watched beside his couch; she had smoothed his pillow and cooled his parched tongue, and bathed his fevered temples; she had been his ministering angel, "and now," thinks Pierre, "what can I do but marry her?"

Mrs. Burkitt was ten years the senior of the little Pierre, and her matronly care-worn aspect, her face traced with the corroding touches of time, to say nothing of the existence of a Mr. Burkitt, did not seem to place her in the line of matrimonial promotion. But what woman ever yet thought herself too old to marry? or, for that matter, too young?

Do not frown my ancient dame, clad in sables; you buried dear John these twenty years ago, and you have grandchildren blooming beside your hearthstone. But do not say, as you hate a falsehood and value the truth, that you are not in the market. You can be bought by a smiling face, or a heavy purse, or a smooth tongue, just as easily now as when you sold out your maiden heart to that rich gawk—your dear, lamented John. If this be not so, why those false teeth; why that shining black braid to obscure the locks of grey; why that padded bosom; why those delicately fashioned lace sleeves; why that immense circumference of skirts; why are you careful to fill up the crow's-feet on your face, and give just a tinge of rouge to those faded cheeks; why that spry walk and that universal simper? Believe it, venerable madam, you are not too old to wear the orange-blossoms. It is not in the power of widowed ladies, or maiden ones either, to arrive at a period of senility when they are unfit for the altar, and the bridal wreath and the honey-moon.

And you, dear little chick—fourteen or thereabouts—just freed from the thralldom of panties and bib and tucker aprons--whose skirts have just been lengthened—

"The future mother swelling in your breast,"

you are not too young to marry; never to young do so good a thing, and isn't it a good thing to secure a home of your own and a protector, even if you do make a foolish man miserable for years by your childish frivolities and inexperiences. No, no! it is best that you should go it while you are young on the high-road to matrimony.

Now Mrs. Burkitt had a woman's heart in her bosom, and that heart was characterized by the usual feminine susceptibilities. Pierre was a handsome little fellow, and would, from his generous impulses, make a good husband. Having suffered so much from a cruel man, why not enjoy some days of happiness with one who promises so fair? This was the woman's argument. It may have been specious, but it was all-sufficient, and though she reserved her emotions, as is the female custom, she felt very tender toward the young Frenchman who had so gallantly and so fondly offered her his heart and hand.

Then followed a gush of tears.

Oh, Pierre! you are done for now. Volatile child of sunny France, you cannot withstand—

> "In woman's eye, the unanswerable tear!
> That weapon of her weakness, which can wield
> To save—subdue—at once her spear and shield!"

There were no further words; but after that day the attentions of Mrs. Burkitt were redoubled.

She had gained the citadel of Pierre's affections, and there she was determined to keep her flag flying. All her cunning arts—her kindnesses—her sighs—her tears—her smiles—all these were brought into play in order to keep the heart of Pierre in subjection.

She knew that it was a man's heart. It might play truant and prove traitorous.

XXI.

HOUSE-RAISING.

PRIOR to leaving Virginia, Dobson Hardy had sent to Richmond, and purchased warrants for one thousand acres of unlocated land. This was in deference to the act of 1781, organizing a land-office, where the depreciated Continental currency was received into the State Treasury in payment for lands in Canetuckey. With the assistance of Kenton, he now set about making a location of his warrant, and finally secured a beautiful tract, combining wood and water, with openings here and there, covered by luxuriant cane.

To build him a cabin, and set up his household gods—his Lares and Penates, was now Dobson's first object.

He accordingly went to work and cleared a sufficient space for a house and garden plat. The situation was chosen in a valley, near the fountain head of a limpid stream, that ran dancing away through the dark woods. Our ancestors were accustomed to select such sites for two reasons: 1st, That they might be near a spring of water. 2d, That they might be in a vale or hollow, as it was easier to take things down to a house than up a hill to it.

The day was appointed for the house-raising, and by dawn, the male inhabitants from far and wide had flocked together to assist in the labors, and participate in the festivities, for such an occasion in those good old times always terminated in a frolic. The mechanical appliances requisite for the construction of a pioneer cabin were few and simple. The logs had already been cut the proper length, and notched at each end where they were to ride each other transversely. A square was laid off, and then the work began. Log after log was raised, and at an altitude of twelve feet there was a pen, in the shape of a parallelogram. The gable-ends were now carried up, with ridge-poles extending lengthwise, for the support of the clap-board roof. These clap-boards—split from oak and poplar timber—were the precursors of shingles, and were laid in regular courses, over each of which a weight-pole was fastened. These poles were retained in their places by short blocks of wood intervening at right angles. The roof completed, a door was cut out, framed, fastened together with wooden pins, and then swung on leathern hinges. Next came the windows. They were small and glass-less, for the glaziers had not yet made their appearance. In lieu, paper, well greased, was used, which admitted a soft and subdued light. Meanwhile two or three of the party have been engaged on the chimney. They have built it broad at the bottom, so that the fire-place may be spacious enough for the family to shelter in. From the foundation it tapers up, a wooden stack of small twigs, so chinked and daubed with mud, that the heat will not affect it. Now they bring flat stones and lay the hearth, and arrange the jambs. Then the slabs split from the oak logs are laid upon the earth, and the puncheon floor is formed.

The cabin is now complete. A dozen industrious, tireless men have labored since sunrise, and their active hands have prepared a home for the new comer. After a while other rooms will be added, as the increasing wants of the family demand them. All that is needed now is, a shelter for the head, and a home hearth-stone about which the family can cluster—a focal place, toward which now, and in all after-time, the hearts of father, mother and children will be drawn as the sweetest place on earth—the *dulce domum* of this life.

And now comes the frolic. Already there is a blue smoke curling from the newly-made chimney, and you will soon discern the odors of savory food. These men have all learned the culinary art by the camp-fires, and are adepts in providing an extempore meal. Dinner at the fashionable hour of sunset is served; a dinner of jole and greens, of corn-cake and buttermilk! The repast finished, the house is illuminated with pine knots, and then fully and finally consecrated to that most unique of all performances—a stag dance!

Didst thou ever participate in one of these exercitations? They are peculiarly and exclusively masculine. Everything wearing the shape or guise of a female is rigidly excluded, and consequently just in proportion as the grace and loveliness of woman is wanting are the innate and natural roughnesses of man apparent. They are not, however, necessarily vulgar, but mere exuberances of genial feelings—the welling over of jolly hearts. Not near so vulgar as that horrid waltz, which even Lord Byron—and he was neither prude or Puritan—reprobated, in stirring verses.

A stag dance is simply a double-shuffle, old-fashioned hoe-down, where you swing your arms and kick with your feet, and shout and laugh and are particularly jovial—with interludes, every few minutes, when the black bottle is handed around, but never passed. It occasionally concludes with a display of pugilism, and exhibitions of maudlin courage, the parties to the dance being generally fuddled, fuzzled, groggy, corned, screwed, raddled, sewed up, lushy, slewed, nappy, muddled, muzzy, and emphatically tight.

But upon this occasion, we are happy to state, there was no such Thracian termination of the festivities.

> "Natis in usum lætitiæ scyphis
> Pugnare Thracum est."

Under the soft light of the stars—in the cool shades of the night—listening to the plaintive cry of the whippoorwill, the happy pioneers ride home, animated by the ecstatic and exulting throb which virtue's votary feels when he sums up the thoughts and actions of a well spent day.

XXII.

HOME.

THE next day Mrs. Hardy went over to take possession of the new home and to assume her duties as mistress of the household. She had already obtained a glimpse of the privations and necessities incident to life in the woods, and was, therefore, not dismayed when she entered the rude cabin. Naturally her mind reverted to the old Virginia home—the spacious rooms, the neat furniture, the broad piazzas, and all the comforts of civilization. She could not refrain from contrasting the two scenes; but the gathering gloom upon her brow, and the sadness in her heart, was dispelled when she saw the smile of Dobson and heard his cheerful voice, and caught the ringing echoes of his axe.

Contracted and rude as was this cabin in the wild wood, and scant as was the furniture, it soon assumed a home aspect. Oh, that gift which women possess of transmuting the merest hovel into an abode of love! How their inspired hands can touch the roughest scenes and shapes, and fashion them into beauty. How their presence, all radiant with purity, can give glory and attraction to the barest log walls.

It will be remembered that all the household effects of the Hardy family were consumed in the destruction of their ark on the battle-night. A new commencement of course had to be made in house-keeping, and as cabinet-makers and furniture dealers did not abound in those days, their wants had to be supplied by the kindness of friends and the ingenuity of an unskilled forest artisan. But here is an inventory of the household and kitchen furniture of a large landholder of Canetuckey in the year 1785, viz.: One bedstead, formed of poplar logs, forked at the top where the cross-pieces were laid; bedding with buffalo robes, deer-skins, and a solitary counterpane; three chairs, whose bottoms were formed of split hickory withes; a table with unhewn legs; a shelf at the door, where the waterpail sat. There was no bureau or sideboard or wardrobe. The dresses and clothing of the family were hung upon wooden pins around the walls, while the cooking and eating utensils were displayed on a mantel over the fire-place. There shone in undiminished splendor the array of pewter plates and dishes, and beside them the irons, spoons and knives and forks, with a full assortment of trenchers, noggins, gourds, etc.

Life in the cabin presented few features of novelty. Day after day it was the same unvarying round; with nights beside the lamp, filled with bear's grease, or at the door watching the stars and engaged in low converse. Thus the time sped on. Mrs. Hardy prepared a neat garden spot, and there she spent pleasant hours, breathing the healthsome odor of the freshly turned soil, and sowing the pea, bean and other vegetables. Nor did she neglect to arrange about each bed of vegetables a bright embroidery of flowers; beside the door she planted a honeysuckle, and it was soon clambering about the window and filling the little room with its rich and grateful perfume. To this odorous El-Dorado the wild bees came humming, and the bumble-bee booming, and the yellow jacket, with his small self full of spite. In the shadowing trees near by the birds built their nests, and the blue-bird, the robin and the wren, during the long summer hours, flitted among the flowers.

And the air was full of life and song as it was full of fragrance.

And the cabin home grew brighter day by day, for it was full of peace and love and content.

XXIII.

ENTANGLED IN THE TOILS OF CUPID.

PIERRE SAVARY was now fully recovered. But still, we much fear that he did not possess that which Cicero deemed so essential: "*Mens sana in corpore sano*"—a sound mind in a sound body. He was whole and perfect in wind and limb; but his heart was sick and sore, and his mental faculties peculiarly perplexed. Mrs. Burkitt had not directly said yea to his violent and enthusiastic protestation of love and offer of hand and heart; but that she was inclined to yield assent, and only delayed according to the custom of her sex, was evident from her continued acts of devotion and tenderness. This uncertain posture of affairs troubled Pierre. He would willingly have been sacrificed then and there as an atonement for his ill-considered haste; but this fluttering in the toils of the net made him restive and uneasy. He felt as if his liberty was restrained, and by degrees he began to beat against the bars of his prison and long for the light, and sunshine, and the freedom without. Marry Mrs. Burkitt he would, though he had discovered, since the films of convalescing gratitude had been removed from his eyes, that she was old enough for his parent. It was a point of honor that he should fulfill his pledge; but, like all Frenchmen, he thought that the ring having been exchanged and the vows recorded, he was disenthralled, and, with the world before him, had the privilege of sucking the sweets from every flower he could find.

Queer, but immutable belief of all French husbands.

His affianced, in the meanwhile, had removed to her sister's, and was there leading a humdrum life, its sameness only relieved when the gallant Pierre stalked through the clearing and presented himself at the cabin threshold, as was his custom on Sabbath mornings. The public ministration of the word of God had, at that time, been introduced to a very limited extent, although in nearly every family the Bible was treasured and the domestic altar reared. On these bright days of rest, while Dobson mused before the door, and the good wife taught her children the Lord's Prayer, and the negroes lay asleep in the sun, the two lovers—shall we call them such?—Pierre and Susanne—for to that French name he bade her answer—strolled through the forests, where, it is to be supposed, they enjoyed halcyon hours of tender communion. Pierre must have been an actor in his Parisian life, for he certainly possessed a tragic air, and these interviews were never concluded without a *dénouement*, the stage effect of which would have been marvellous.

And thus their weeks were crowned with blissful Sundays, until on one occasion, early in the autumn, when, to the unrevealing trees, there was added another spectator of these dramatic scenes.

Mrs. Hardy had completed the usual scrip tural lesson, and while awaiting the preparation of the evening meal, walked out into the forest. She soon heard the sound of voices—then the rustle of the falling leaves and the crackling of a dry twig. Half frighted she turned to flee, when what should the amazed woman see! No panther with glaring eyes, nor stealthily treading Indian. The curtain had risen upon the last act of the afternoon melodrama. Pierre had just thrown himself in a kneeling posture before Mrs. Burkitt, and with uplifted hands, and appealing face, and frenzied eyes, and flowing locks, presented as pretty a piece of pantomimic despair as one could wish to see on or off the stage.

Startled, dumbfounded, astonished and overwhelmed, Mrs. Hardy returned to the cabin, having escaped observation. She was a woman of policy, and knew that it would not be proper to make any sudden revelation of her discovery, nor indulge in any outburst of surprise and indignation. The twain, little imagining that their secret had been revealed, returned in the softened twilight, and were greeted as usual. Indeed, if there were any change perceptible in the deportment of the housewife, it was in an increase of her geniality.

Schooled to betray no emotions when she desired they should be hidden, she talked through the evening in a light vein of pleasantry, while her heart was trembling with the shock it had sustained from the unexpected forest disclosure. Her heart, did we say—better have said her sense of propriety, for by the fitness of things most women regulate their feelings.

XXIV.

A HUNTING EXCURSION.

THE autumn was well advanced. Hardy had successfully used the bright summer weather in preparing his farm for the next year's crops; he had already quite a number of acres under fence, and the trees upon a large area were girdled, so that in the spring he could commence farming on a somewhat extensive scale. Additions and comforts had also been made to his house, and it was now both commodious and attractive. His wife had not only become reconciled to the forest life, but such had been the cloudless splendor of the summer and fall, so propitious every occurrence and so prosperous their circumstances, that she was thankful her lot had been cast where fortune seemed destined to shower upon them its golden blessings.

In the various cabin homes and stations of

that section, preparations were being made for the usual annual hunt. Of course Dobson joined in the expedition. He was the more ready to leave home ; from the security that had prevailed the past year: no Indian signs having been seen in that time, and he well knew that his negroes, Tom and Cash, would guard well and hold out bravely against any attack, should one be made.

The day came around for the hunters to depart on their excursion—there were thirteen of them, all on foot, with their rifles, shot-pouches and knapsacks slung over their shoulders—fleet of foot, every one of them a

πόδας ωκὺς 'Αχίλλεύς

—they did not require the assistance of horses to keep pace with the flying deer. Nevertheless they took several of those faithful animals to bear home the game they might capture; and although their acute and trained instincts in tracing the objects of their sport, almost rendered the employment of dogs unnecessary, still, every man was attended with two or three canines—most of them curs of low degree. A day's tramp through the pathless woods, and they arrive at the hunting-ground. There they prepare their half-faced cabin, as a place of general rendezvous. This was formed with a large log for its back—eight or ten feet in front a couple of stakes were driven, from these the roof sloped toward the back, and was covered with slabs, skins and bark. The front was left entirely open, and there the fire was built, while the hunters sheltered themselves within, their feet resting in the hot ashes as they slept—a sure precaution against rheumatism.

Each morning the hunters were accustomed to sally out in pairs, returning at night to headquarters, where they feasted on a sumptuous supper of bear and venison, accompanied by buffalo steaks, and that most nutritious and delicious bread—the johnny-cake, baked upon a board in the ashes. Then, gathering by the watch-fire, they recounted the adventures of the day, and the signs of the woods.

To be a successful hunter required very uncommon attributes of body and mind. Besides personal powers and ability to undergo great hardships, the understanding must be comprehensive, the apprehension ready and the judgment decided. There was no time for hesitancy in an encounter with a ferocious bear, or in the pursuit of the antlered monarch of the forest. Steadiness of aim, a practised eye, a nerved arm, and the finger never too quick upon the trigger, were essential qualifications. There was also a certain species of woodcraft in which the hunter must be versed. He must be able to read the weather, and tell from the sky where the game was to be found. He must know from experience that in stormy weather the deer always seek the sheltered places, and the leeward sides of the hills—that in rainy weather, when there is not much wind, they keep in the open woods and on the highest ground. It was essential that the hunter should not only be a barometer and thermometer, but possess the ability of ascertaining the direction of the wind, so as to be enabled to regulate his movements. For this purpose he was accustomed to place his finger in his mouth until it was warmed, and then raising it above his head, the side of his finger which first became cold would tell him the course of the wind, and the direction of the chase would be in accordance with this singularly obtained information. The points of the compass, too, were as necessary in the waste of woods, as on that of water. The appearance of the bark and moss on the trunks of trees very accurately determined for them the navigation of the forest. The bark of an aged tree is always much thicker on the north side.

Kenton and Hardy, who were partners in the first day's hunt, had been each successful in putting a ball through the shoulders of a deer, besides killing lesser game, and toward dusk were preparing for a return to the camp, when the former descried bear tracks in the light snow which had fallen the previous night. Following up the trail, although it was now almost night, they came to the creek where the thin skin of ice had been but recently broken. In a ledge of rocks on the opposite shore, was the mouth of a cave, where the animal had evidently taken refuge. Hardy was indisposed to pursue the game any further, being wearied with the day's work; but Kenton, who seemed never to be satisfied while there was a wild beast or a wild Indian within reach, insisted on adding this trophy to the spoils of the hunt. They accordingly crossed the stream; after reconnoitering a few moments, Simon observed that "the bar was right thar in the cave, shore." "How do you know that?" asked Hardy.

"Why," responded the sagacious and experienced hunter: "don't you see the last tracks made are with the toe-marks toward the cave? And thar's only one of 'em, 'case the tracks are regl'ar, and of the same size, and he's a monstrous big 'un, judgin' by the length of the step, and the size of the paws, and he's a duced fat feller, fur don't you see his hind feet don't step on the tracks made by the fore ones, as would be the case if he war a lean bar. Now, man, you've never slayed one these fellers, s'pose you try your hand on."

If Dobson had spoken out like an honest and candid man he would have confessed his reluctance to an encounter with the bear; but unwilling to be regarded in any other light than a hazardous, adventurous person, he expressed to Kenton his intense desire to enter the cave and demolish the huge animal.

Kenton was too excellent a judge of human nature not to discover that this was affected enthusiasm on the part of his companion; but he thought it as fitting opportunity as any to teach him a lesson, and he accordingly praised the courage and spirit of Dobson, until the latter really felt as if he was a very spirited sort of individual. Instructing him how to proceed, Kenton lighted a candle made of beeswax, and placing it in Dobson's hand, pushed him into the cave, with an injunction to be steady and fire at the eyes. Entering into the midnight darkness, which the flickering light of the candle only rendered the more visible, Dobson crawled along carefully, and finally placed the light in the seam of a rock, and waited the movements of the bear. He soon saw a huge, black mass moving at the remote end of the cave. It was the animal which had been disturbed by the glare of the candle-light. Slowly he walked forward to ascertain the occasion of this disturbance in his Erebian realm. The hunter lay flat on the bottom of the cave watching the progress of the bear. When within a few yards of the candle he fired, straight at the eyes, but the aim was not correct, and the ball only flattened against the adamantine shoulder-blade of the animal. He had no time to re-load before the bear would be up to him, and how could he possibly contend in a hand to hand encounter with such a terrible opponent? He would retreat and become a butt for the jeers of his companions, but he could not do that before the bear would be on him. It was a desperate crisis. In a moment Bruin, foaming with rage, was confronting the trembling Dobson, and with one blow of his huge paw had dashed the uplifted knife from the hands of the hunter, and was about encircling him in a deadly embrace, when bang went a rifle, and the huge brute fell to the ground an inanimate heap. The bullet had actually cut the fox-tail with which Dobson's cap was ornamented, and then entering the eye of the bear, had penetrated the brain, causing instant death.

Kenton, who was anxious to test the grit of Dobson, had followed him into the cave, and just at the important moment his steady nerve and never-failing aim had released him from what appeared to be certain death.

Placing the immense carcass where it could be secured on the morrow, and cutting off the paws, as evidences of their prowess, the hunters emerged from the cave, and although the night was pitch dark, it was bright in contrast with the subterranean gloom from which they had just emerged.

XXV.

HOW LOVE'S YOUNG DREAM WAS DISSIPATED.

ONE Saturday evening, while Mr. Hardy was absent on his hunting excursion, the two sisters were sitting silently before the fire, engaged with their own thoughts, and apparently unobservant of the dancing, flickering, ever-changing lights and shadows upon the walls—the glittering showers of sparks and the red tongues of flame which lapped up the dry wood as if they were thirsting for fuel.

Suddenly Mrs. Hardy turned her eyes from the white ashes, where they may have been conjuring the phantoms of dead joys and sorrows, and fixing her gaze upon Mrs. Burkitt, said in her usual clear, cold tones:

"Sister Susan, I must tell you one thing I have wrongly neglected informing you of heretofore, as I thought that amidst your multiplied sorrows it would not be proper to thrust another care upon your already overburdened heart. But doubtless it would have been best had I unfolded the whole dreadful truth to you at the start, for by this time you might have entirely recovered your peace of mind."

Mrs. Burkitt started when she heard her sister's voice, and the threatened revelation of some new calamity caused her to gasp as if she were struggling for breath. She could but articulate, indistinctly and brokenly: "What now? Has God reserved other judgments for me?"

"No! No other judgment. I have only to tell you that your husband—God be merciful to him—lives, or did, just as we were leaving Virginia!"

She then detailed all the incidents narrated at the opening of our sketch, with painful minuteness.

The poor woman, more than a widowed sufferer, listened with interest, but manifested no outward sign of excitement. It was enough for her to know that *he* lived—that he had been suffering—that Providence was not yet weary chastising him. In a moment all her old affection rushed back and she clasped the old idol to her breast. Her heart, that had been warmed by a new passion, relapsed into its former condition of patient sufferance.

The next day was the Sabbath, and with it came Pierre—for, poor fellow, he was fairly fascinated, and unable to remain for more than a week at a time without the magic circle, although he had repeatedly resolved to try the effects of absence on his consuming passion.

The air was raw; the sky drear; the woods bare. No time now for quiet walks and secret conferences and extempore acting. But Mrs. Hardy knew what would be the result of to-day's meeting, and she left the couple alone for an hour, that what she had planned might be executed.

When all alone, Mrs. Burkitt, who was now quite resigned, said calmly to Pierre:

"This confidential intercourse of ours must not continue any longer. It is very pleasant, and you are a kind and amiable man. But I have a husband living whom I thought dead. It was not known to me until last night. So we must part, but always, I hope, continue friends!"

Really, we believe, the little Frenchman would have exceeded himself in tragic deportment had he not been detained in his place by the cold and glittering eye of Mrs. Burkitt. He only snatched her hand and pressed it passionately to his lips, and without uttering a word, either of grief or expostulation, sank back into his chair, hissing between his teeth a sacr-r-r-r-e!

And thus ended Pierre's love-making with the woman old enough to be his mother.

In a few moments the table was spread, the steaming bowl of mush and milk was introduced, the fragrant herb tea bubbled in an iron kettle, the remnants of a cold possum looked appetizing, and the pone of corn bread smelt as sweet as a harvest field. They all supped, talking quietly and then gathered about the fire.

Pierre rose to leave; but Mrs. Hardy, going to the door, looked out and said the clouds were full of snow, that the wind was soughing through the trees as if it were a lost spirit, and that it would not do for him to ride home that night. He was prevailed upon to remain.

We have remarked before that Mrs. Hardy was a politic woman. She had overheard—accidentally, of course—the brief conversation between her sister and Pierre. If they were to separate now, with the memory of the parting sadly fresh in their hearts, evil might result. It would be best to disenchant them now and forever. Thus she reasoned and acted. Reasoned and acted well.

XXVI.

SALT-MAKING AT THE BLUE LICKS.

PIERRE went back to his salt-making and soon forgot the love dream in which he had tossed through months of incertitude and conflicting sentiments.

A man of some scientific attainments and considerable ingenuity, he had suggested various improvements in the manufacture of salt at the Blue Licks, where that article was then principally prepared, and his advice had proven so profitable that he was installed as superintendent. With the aid of three negroes he managed to produce a supply adequate for the wants of the various settlements. But the means of production were so limited, and the saline principles in the water so few, that it took a first-rate man to be worth his salt in those days; the article in the rough selling at eight dollars per hundred.

The process used in evaporation was quite simple. A pit some four feet deep and about forty feet in length was dug, where huge fires were kindled. Over these about twenty brazen pots, of the capacity of ten gallons each, were arranged and filled with water from the numerous springs, as the occasion required. The chief labor was in supplying wood to feed the furnaces, an enormous amount of fuel being daily and nightly consumed.

For how many centuries we know not, these licks had been the resort of buffalo, elk, deer, and other animals, who came from all sections to taste the waters and lick the earth which was so thoroughly impregnated with salt. Traces leading to the place, worn smooth and hard as the old Appian Way, by the constant tread of myriads of beasts, converged from every point of the compass, and the land, for a wide area in the immediate vicinity of the springs, was as bare and destitute of vegetation as the thunder stricken summit of an Alpine peak.

These salt works were long ago deserted; but the Blue Licks were destined to be the gathering place of others beside these quadrupedal hordes. We wonder if our little Pierre, when seated before the boiling salt-kettles, the bleak landscape and the midnight darkness only relieved by the blazing fires, ever dreamed of the metamorphosis that time would work in the scenes of his labors. Could he but have looked into the future he would have beheld the giddy throngs of fashion flaunting about that drear spot—poor, feeble, tottering invalids, seeking the restoration of health—pure young girls, with hearts to lose, entering the mazes of society, and losing hearts and all! He might have beheld fortunes staked at the gaming table, and Vice holding its summer carnival. But he would have seen that Beauty and Innocence were not entire strangers in the brilliant saloons, and along the sequestered mountain paths, and on the bosom of the gently flowing Licking.

XXVII.

THE SUGAR-CAMP.

THE first winter in the wilderness was passed, not without its discomforts; but these were more than atoned for by the pleasures incident to that season of storm. Then it is, indeed, that the better nature of man bourgeons and blossoms in all its fullness, and nowhere do little, but hearty acts of kindness, manifest themselves as peculiarly as in a remote settlement where the resources of social enjoyment are limited, and the exercise of the rites of friendship and companionableness are attended by risk and danger. Throughout the dreary months there had been merry-makings, feastings, frolics, hunts and all those pastimes significant of hearts that the winter's cold could not chill, and generous blood which could not be checked in its warm and passionate currents, by any of the icy restraints of climate.

Partridges, those delicious, juicy and plump winged companions of civilization—never being found save in proximity to white settlements—were to be trapped. After each fall of snow the timid rabbits were tracked to their burrows. There was not a gum-tree but revealed the domicile of a possum. Thus an abundance of healthful, honest, exhilarating out-door sport was afforded the pioneers, while the shroud of winter wrapped their landed possessions.

Within doors there was no lack of employment for the brisk housewives. Merrily hummed the spinning-wheels; clatter, clatter went the looms; stitch, stitch into the new garments and old rents. There was cooking, and serving, and all the duties of domesticity, winter as well as summer.

Thus the days, so very brief and dark, were lengthened with pleasures and brightened with merriment, and the grim winter passed away like any other shadow.

The mornings were now cool and clear, with a frostiness in the air, that tingled the cheek and quickened the step, and flushed the spirits like a cup of old Crow. Just the time for sugar-making. Now the maple is brimming with its sweet juices, and yonder, in the thick woods, where there are spiral columns of smoke, and the fire flashes its red light through the shadowy grove, and the voices of youth and happiness ring out like the chimes of silver bells—over bubbling kettles of sirup hang the faces of the wood nymphs, their eyes sparkling and their lips pouting and their round cheeks glowing. The golden liquid simmers and sputters, sending forth its saccharine vapors until the whole camp is redolent of sweet savors. Active young men tap the blackened old trees, and tend the troughs, and replenish the kettles with sugar-water, and keep the fires blazing. The labor is forgotten in the pleasurable excitement, and all sense of wearinees is banished by the joy that buoys every heart and brightens every footstep and lightens every load.

XXVIII.

THE BENCH OF MAGISTRATES.

AND now Spring had come once again, fresh from the hidden caverns of perfume, and as she trode the earth with her warm and delicate feet, the flowers and the birds awoke, and the farmer, looking abroad over his fields, regirt his loins for the campaign which would result in golden sheaves and a happy harvest home. How lovely looked all the land in its fresh, green robes. How fragrant the bloom of the wild clover which here grew in native luxuriance. How bright and glossy the tall and slender reeds of cane, full of succulence, springing up everywhere in original vigor. How delicious the song of the robin as he builds his home in the tree-top, and the swallows twittering about the eaves.

The tide of emigration had already set in.

Daily ark after ark landed at Limestone, and the roads soon became populous with the thronging multitudes who where seeking new homes in the wilderness. These indications of prosperity were most cheering, and every fresh arrival from the States was hailed by the old settlers with unbounded manifestations of joy. The northern part of Fayette had just been formed into a separate county, and styled Mason, in honor of one of the most glorious spirits of Virginia. Its boundaries were extensive, embracing all the country from the mouth of the Licking to the Big Sandy, and bounded by the Licking at the south. For the seat of justice of this new county, Simon Kenton donated William Wood and Arthur Fox one thousand acres of land lying near his station. There these two men located the town of Washington, which almost immediately became a thriving place. Little did the gallant and generous Kenton imagine then that this noble gift would cause him days and months of anxiety, and that even upon the very land he had given for the site of the temple of Justice, he would be held in bonds—the victim of the grossest injustice from those he had benefited.

The commissions for the magistrates had arrived. They were sealed with the great seal of Virginia, and signed by Benjamin Harrison, the Governor, with the same bold dash of the pen that he had used when affixing his name to the Declaration of Independence. Court could not now be held too soon. The peace and the dignity of the public demanded that the scales of Justice should be arranged for balancing the rights and wrongs of the community. There was no court-house—for that was years before the glorious old stone-hammer's time—and a room had to be fitted up in Basil Burgess' tavern, as the temporary abode of the blind goddess. Here the high priests at her altar—four blooming, stout, self-satisfied, blue-eyed men—looking as if they had been chosen on account of their mutual resemblance, assembled and inaugurated the career of jurisprudence in that part of Kentucky. It was a goodly sight. The air of pomp with which they entered, the dignity with which they arranged their flowing robes, the magisterial grace with which they stroked their long cues—these impressed the people, who had seen nothing so grand out of the old State. It is true that they had witnessed battalions of mounted men, hastening with the sound of trumpets and clangor of arms, to some Indian foray, but these spectacles were not to be compared in impressiveness with the owl-like deportment and oracular looks and gowned weightiness and powdered heads of a bench of magistrates. Somehow or other this has ever been the case. A conclave of solemn owls would awe you more than the lightning swoop of a fierce-voiced eagle. Indeed half the utility of courts consists, not in their utterances and actions, but in their dignified reserve of powers and attributes, which the people in their ignorance invest with an awful solemnity, that is farcical to those persons (lawyers, for instance) who know how shallow are all the tricks of the legal trade.

The crier proclaims the court open with his resonant "OYEZ," and his official prayer for the salvation of the commonwealth.

"What case have you, Mr. Attorney?'

"May it please your honors, Wm. Lightfoot is charged with stealing a flitch of bacon from Lucas Sullivant."

The proof is heard, and Lightfoot is sentenced to receive thirteen stripes on the bare back—that number being awarded him in honor of the number of States in the confederation.

John Naylor is arraigned for stealing certain edge tools from Slack and Pyle. Guilty and sentenced to thirty-nine lashes, well laid on, as provided in the Mosaic code.

Now a burly negro is presented. Dick, a slave of Thomas Brooks, has stolen two yards and three quarters of cambric from Wm. Goforth, jr. Proof heard in ten minutes—a buzz of consultation between the magistrates—a glance at Henning's statutes—the court agrees upon a verdict, and Squire Lee announces that for this theft Dick must be hung on the 4th day of June. And he was hung between the blue heaven and the green earth in the bright sunshine of that June day. So were many other negroes at other times, for like petty offences. That was before Jefferson had concluded his revisal of the code of Virginia—tempering those cruel laws with mercy, and infusing into the administration of the courts a benignity and humanity which had been before wholly foreign to them.

But we have not time to go through with all the cases. Richard McClure is fined five hundred pounds of tobacco for divulging false news, and Robert Wilson, having just now spoken disrespectfully to John Machir, gentleman and

Justice, is fined for this breach of good manners in presence of an honorable dignitary of the State.

Court is proclaimed adjourned. The magistrates doff their official robes, but none of their dignified, imposing mien. Marching down into the tavern bar-room they seat themselves, and calling for their toddies, drink libation after libation to Justice, whose ministers they are.

And thus the law is administered for the first time north of the Licking River. There are court-houses and judges in abundance there now; but we daresay that were all the judicial officials of this anno Domini lumped together, their good sense, good manners, and zeal and strictness in business would not overbalance that of the four rosy cheeked, tippling, swearing squires of lang syne.

XXIX.

THE DREADFUL BLOW.

"WEEL, we had a braw time to-day, friend Dobson. There was sic a cannie youth from the old State, who spoke from the stump on the green common. I vow his arguments were strong, and he demonstrated to a certainty that your great friend Wilkinson is after no good in his dealings and traffickings with the Spaniards. He said, and I agree with him too, that we should adhere to the old State, and when the proper time comes then we can peaceably secede with her consent, and become one of the confederacy. That's what he said was the feeling in Virginia, and I think it's what it ought to be here."

"Pshaw, Campbell, you don't understand the merits of this question. Here we are unprotected by the parent government—separated from them hundreds of miles by frowning mountains and a gloomy wilderness. We owe them nothing for the past, for we have built up our own prosperity, and we have defended ourselves, as we shall have to do yet, with blood and treasure. Then we have no outlet for our surplus produce, except over the mountains, and the Federal Congress will not interfere to secure the right of free navigation of the Mississippi, which was years ago stipulated in a treaty. Now Spain offers to allow us to trade down the river; will buy our tobacco, and corn, and flour, and will, besides, afford us sufficient protection. I am for General Wilkinson's scheme. He is a true man and brave soldier. I knew him at Princeton, where he fought most gallantly, as indeed he did throughout the wars. He is a man who loves his country."

"Ah! can a person truly love his country and sell that country at the same time for Spanish gold, as this Wilkinson is doing? Don't his pockets jingle with the yellow doubloons whenever he comes this way, and isn't he always receiving great piles of specie from Low Louisiana? Bless my eyes, who do I see riding there through the woods? If it isn't the young man who spoke to-day at Washington. See, Dobson, his glossy black horse, and how he sits him like a Centaur!"

Sure enough, there came dashing up the path a mettlesome steed, coal black, and gracefully formed, surmounted by a young man whose flow of animal spirits seemed as exuberant—judging by the almost audible smile that wreathed his face, and the abandon with which he rode—as those of the noble horse he bestrode.

He did not hail the house, as was the custom of the country, nor salute Dobson and Campbell, who were seated in the front stoop, smoking their cob-pipes, as strangers. Leaping from his horse, with agile step he was in a moment before the astonished pioneers, clasping Dobson with an affectionate embrace, which startled that undemonstrative man.

One tone of his deep, rich voice, and one glance into the depths of his burning eye, satisfied Dobson who his visitor was. But speech utterly failed him when he attempted to frame words of welcome. His happiness at meeting an old and gallant friend, and the sorrowful remembrances which that meeting awakened, combined to palsy his voice. He could but look unutterable satisfaction and wring the young man's hands with his mighty grasp.

The staid Scotchman, unable to comprehend so violent and enthusiastic a dumb greeting, and fearing that his presence might interfere with the complete satisfaction of the two re-united friends, strayed through the shaded yard, his course marked by the clouds of smoke which were whiffed from his pipe, and curled about his head in fantastic shapes.

Dobson could readily detect in the earnest and longing glances that the new comer directed toward the door, that he was not at all satisfied thus to loiter on the threshold of long-anticipated bliss. Without a word he led him within; but just beyond the door-sill they encountered Mrs. Hardy. At the sight of Basil Greene the fountains of her heart seemed broken up. Yielding to the cordial embrace, she gave way to a flood of tears—tears from the depths of a divine despair.

Basil was unable to account for this singular reception. Had not his heart been so full of fond anticipation—had not the longing lover usurped the place of the keen-eyed man of business, he might have read in the manner and emotions of these two worthy people the painful truth which was so soon to fall like a cursed blight upon his hopes.

They were seated in the best room, and Dobson, glad to be rid of the unpleasant scene, had left Basil alone with his wife. After the first great passion had subsided, she resumed her accustomed passive manner, and the keenest scrutinizer of those cold and pallid features could not have detected any traces of the recent stormy grief that had swept over her soul. Even after regaining her self-possession, she remained silent, nerving herself for the proper control of her voice.

Just then there was a rustle of skirts beside the door, and a light step. Basil turned instinctively, eager to catch the first glimpse, and prompt to clasp to his own breast the form which he had last seen fading away from him in the Virginian twilight.

Up spoke Mrs. Hardy in her clear, cold tones —mercilessly and bitterly cold they seemed to that listener:

"You need not look, Basil; you will never see her more! Poor Mary is not here!"

"Not here—never see her again!" shrieked

Basil, recoiling from the bearer of these tidings, and shivering at her words of ice.

"Can she be dead?" he muttered in a monotone, and then, as the even more dreadful supposition recurred to him, that, perhaps, she had forgotten her troth and bestowed her heart elsewhere, he summoned all his courage and kept back the stammering, broken sentences which would have shown too plainly how utterly his heart was crushed.

"Yes, she is dead," said this most imperturbable woman; and not stopping to notice the pallor that spread over Basil's cheek, nor to observe how his sturdy frame quivered as an aspen, nor to heed his gasping queries as he clutched at portions of her narrative, she proceeded to detail, in her frigid manner, all the circumstances attending the sudden and mysterious disappearance of Mary.

Perhaps it were better thus to have the stories of our great calamities unfolded to us by a calm, disciplined friend, in whose voice you can detect no tremor, in whose narrative there are only bald words and no touches of pathos, no sympathy, no condolence, no sharing of the cup of the sorrow. It may be that you can thus the sooner realize your forlorn and stricken condition. Nevertheless, in an hour of misery and gloom, let us see the tender glance and feel the comforting touch. If some dreadful, sorrowful truth is to be revealed to us, let the voice that tells the saddening tale be warm and gentle and soothing, and even broken by sobs.

When the sad truth had been fully told, Basil did not utter those words of Scripture which had been so consoling to the mother and aunt under similar afflicting circumstances. He could not find it in his heart to say: "God doeth all things well." Had he not for months looked forward to the day of meeting? Had it not ever loomed forward in the sky of his future, no matter what clouds or gloom obscured? Faithful to the end —ah! bitter end it seemed now—had he not kept his heart pure and blameless and unseduced, that he might bring it as a spotless tribute to the woman of his choice? To win her approving smiles had he not struggled and toiled—had he not endured privations—had he not overcome mountains—had he not fought legions of adversaries, and in every contest with the doubts and fears that would assail him, had he not proven the victor? He had loved and striven, and patiently suffered, and now was he to be thus cast down? Were all his hopes to be thus ruthlessly destroyed, and the smiling face of the heavens blotted out from his vision forever?

It was too cruel a blow, and his heart rebelled against the great Chastener, and when Mrs. Hardy whispered that precious text, he mockingly scoffed at the teachings of a being who could thus smite and then offer mere words as consolation. Rebellion naturally created distrust, and the poor sufferer, whose mind had never been fully enlightened concerning the ways of Providence, in his madness and misery doubted the wisdom and justice of the God of his fathers. He spoke bitterly against the Creator, who having made man, and placed him in a paradise, then purposely planted the tree of evil, so that he might eat and perish, thus sating His malice. He scoffed in his incoherent ravings at the great plan of salvation. It was but a narrow scheme, enabling the few who are marked and elect to credit the strange sacrifice of the Son, and thus save their souls; while millions shall live and die, never hearing the Saviour's name, and hence go to the gaping grave unredeemed. Was this justice?

For days Basil lay in a trance, now and then waking for a moment, and calling upon Mary, wildly, madly, passionately. Then, in other intervals of his death-like sleep, he would rave as any madman, and words of blasphemy, which before had never polluted his lips, would roll forth in the vehemence of his unnatural anger. He cursed earth and heaven and hell—all things and all beings, with a violence that was shocking.

The faithful women never deserted him. Tenderly they tended beside his couch, and strove, as only women know how, to alleviate his distresses. But could they minister to a mind diseased? Better, believe it, than would be imagined. The patient, gentle, uncomplaining, pensive face of a woman, bending over the couch of the delirious, is certain to reflect inwardly upon the sufferer. No matter whether a bright, unsullied young face, or one that has been stamped with years of suffering. Let the woman only be good. Heaven has writ upon the faces of all good women a message of hope and love, whose cheering words flash upon us in straits of illness and despair.

Basil had thus been brought through the crisis

of a severe illness. These two good souls, without the aid of doctors, had led him gently through the darkened valley up to the blessed mountain-heights of health. Mrs. Burkitt, when she heard of the attachment between the sufferer and her daughter, felt a maternal affection for him, and gave up her days and nights to vigils at his couch.

Restored, but not to complete health, and feeling, as the tide of life once more ebbed and flowed through his veins, how blessed it is to live, Basil began to cast about him for occupation, for he knew that his mind, weakened and shattered, must have some employment to distract it from wretched thoughts and sad memories.

XXX.

THE GOSPEL IN THE WILDERNESS.

OF this June Sabbath, the words of old George Herbert are the fittest description:

> "Sweet day, so cool, so calm, so bright,
> The bridall of the earth and skies."

There was to be religious worship some eight miles from the Hardy home, and thither the family, servants and all, were bound. Horses were saddled and bridled at an early hour, and soon they were clattering along the shaded forest road. As they proceeded, they joined other parties on horseback, and overtook scores who were trudging on foot. It was considered nothing then to walk a dozen miles to hear the preaching of the blessed Word.

After a pleasant ride through fields green with the ripening harvest, and woods surcharged with the melody of birds and the perfume of nodding flowers—beside new homes that were springing up in neighborly nearness—across brooks that, to the sleeping woods, all night sing a quiet tune—they reached the scene of the day's services. It was an immense tract of woodland, clear of undergrowth, and the green sward as smooth and neat as if trimmed for the occasion. The woods were already populous with worshippers, and from the centre of the throng there arose the hum of melody; at first low and indistinct, then bursting out in full harmonious numbers, until the very leaves quivered, and the deep, rich music rolled through the forest, and across the valleys, and up, up to the sky, where it was blent with the blessed song of angels.

A rude stand had been erected, and about it hewn logs were placed at regular intervals, affording seats for many hundreds. The preacher mounts the rustic pulpit and announces this text—it is that brief verse in the Gospel of John: "Jesus wept." At once the multitude fix their eyes upon the speaker, and for two hours (those were not the days of pleasant little forty-minute discourses) the listeners are riveted to their seats. They lean forward, anxious that not one word of the precious message shall escape them. The preacher's voice is melodious, his accents pure, and his words gentle and persuasive. His manners are a happy composite of the frank and out-spoken style of the woods, and the ease and grace of the city. His thoughts are marked by long communion with nature, and yet give evidence of the polish of books. Evidently he has seen much of life in its various phases. He has dwelt among libraries, and drawn power and strength from the old masters of theology. He has spent months in the wilderness, studying its rugged forms and finding inspiration in that great fountain source which avails him here when he would speak pointedly and plainly—when he would strike home to the hearts and consciences of these backwoods people; he has learned their modes of thought and speech, and he uses their expressive and somewhat blunt phraseology, without sacrificing purity of diction; he knows their boldness and chivalry; he is likewise bold and chivalrous; he finds he can best influence their feelings by sharing with them their dangers and trials; he is a foremost man in the hunt; he shrinks from no perilous undertaking; he falters not when the arrows of death are whizzing through the air; he rushes through the gloom, and fury, and blackness of tempests; he knows that God is everywhere and ever mindful, and that by demonstrating his own perfect reliance on the strong arm of the Almighty, he can best draw others to the same great rock of defence and security.

Such were the tactics of the pioneer preachers; such the requirements of the men who first lifted the standard of the cross in the western wilds. Strong were their hands and strong their hearts, and strongest of all, their faith in the Lord Jesus Christ. They were not delicate, thin-voiced men, but Boanerges; each one of them a son of thunder; they did not poetize, and dream, and articulate in lisping syllables essays upon love and morality, as do most of the modern divines; they did not discourse upon politics, but found more fitting themes in the wondrous events of their Saviour's life—in the higher concerns of immortality; they made the world and men better by the impressive lessons they taught, and by the pure, bold, manly lives they led.

Basil soon discovered that the preacher had thrown a spell over him; nor was he at all anxious to dissolve it. The subject was one full of interest at all times, in all places, and to all men. Its lessons were especially pertinent to the mental condition of Basil. The sufferings, the agony, the woe, the misery, and above all, the tender, loving, affectionate kindness of Jesus, were depicted in the most striking light. The hand which drew these scenes in his life and presented that pathetic picture of the Saviour weeping at the tomb of Lazarus, was not feeble Every stroke of the pencil was masterly, and the broad canvas, as it was unfurled, glowed with the effective touches of the mighty artist, who, there in the wilderness, with his pencil of flame, could paint upon the impalpable air scenes that brought tears, and aroused erring hearts, and startled men in their wayward ways, and pointed to heaven, to that Mediator who had here wept in the agony of his distress over the sinfulness of fallen man. Every heart in the large throng caught the sympathatic glow of the speaker. Tears suffused their eyes as they gazed upon the picture of Christ's agony for sinning humanity, and remembered his great condescension in suffering that the world might live.

Thus for two hours the people held their places in rapt attention. At the conclusion of the sermon they united as one man in singing the old hymn:

> "Jesus my all to heaven has gone"—

singing it not with the mere artistic skill of trained choristers, but with what is much better, the spirit and the understanding—framing with their golden words of praise and music a way of ascent to the ear of the Father.

Then followed the noon repast. Each family had brought with it provisions for the dinner-hour, and gathering in groups beneath the overhanging trees, white cloths were spread upon the smooth grass, and the happy people regaled themselves with their substantial food.

After this brief intermission the people collected again to hear another of their favorite teachers. There was a striking difference in the two sermons, and it would have been difficult to have determined which best satisfied the hearers. That of the morning was pungent and effective in arousing their hearts—in appealing to their sympathies—in startling them with the wide gulf between their ways of sin and the paths of peace and pleasantness, where true wisdom trod. It was consoling also, as it presented Jesus in that most affecting of possible positions, sharing the grief and sorrow of poor fallen humanity, for the loss of one of its number. Thus there was naturally deduced the kindness and gentleness of a system which, while it was strict and even stern in its requirements, was tempered by mercy and consecrated by all-pervading love.

The afternoon discourse was a calm, dispassionate argument, demonstrating God's justice in all things. It was a solid, compact piece of reasoning, unadorned by rhetoric and unrelieved a single gleam of pity. That God doeth all things well—that the sinner would certainly meet his doom and the elect Christian his reward—that no leaf fell, no harvest was blighted, no station overwhelmed with murder and fire at midnight, but in the course of God's overruling Providence. There was no tenderness of thought—not a spark of feeling—not a tremor of the voice denoting emotion. Like that rugged old metaphysician, our American Jonathan Edwards, this backwoods evangelist, in his discourse deilberately carried his hearers to the very verge of hell, and bade them look in; but not the whole heat of its burnings could melt into a tear the ice in his eye. He bade them gaze upon a great portion of their fellow men stretched through eternity upon a wheel of torture, but his eyelids quivered no more than if he looked upon a butterfly. It was only when at the mouth of this gaping hell he bade them listen to the melodies of heaven, that he varied in the least from the unimpassioned coldness of his ratiocination.

Such was the preaching our fathers enjoyed. It was strong meat, and built them up in a faith that all the winds and storms of unbelief and heresy could never disturb.

You will not hear such messages from your pulpit next Sabbath. Our ministers have given up that kind of earnest, effective discourse. They deal now in essays; they preach statistics; they quote poetry; they make sensation hits; they deliver lectures, but never preach; they offer the blue skim-milk of the Gospel diluted with water, for the nourishment of the babes of Israel. No wonder. The Christians of this age would revolt at the presentation of such doctrinal food as that upon which their fathers thrived and strengthened.

But with these two sermons, a faint echo of which we have attempted to give, the exercises of the day were not complete. There were yet other duties to perform. Near by was a running stream, and, as at Ænon near Salim, there was much water there. Thither the entire congregation wended their way, and grouping along the gently sloping banks of the creek, they witnessed the ordinance of baptism administered. First an elderly man was led into the water, where he submitted to the administration. Next a young girl, in the ripening beauty and fresh innocence of her glad life. And then a swarthy negro, the very one indeed whose fate was so recently and summarily decided by the bench of magistrates. He is under condemnation of death, but has been allowed the privilege of religious instruction, and brought here to-day, under guard, that he might be enabled to publicly profess his faith. It was a sad and solemn, as well as unusual, spectacle. The doomed victim, strengthened by inward faith, and the hopes of a better hereafter, stepped firmly into the stream, and bowed his head beneath the crystal wave, the voice of hundreds uniting in that baptismal hymn:

"In all my Lord's appointed ways."

Then the communicants were seated upon the grassy bank, and with the golden sunset floating on them between the trees, kissing the water, and crowning, as with a halo, the head of the minister who blessed the sacraments, these people of God—there in the howling wilderness—partook of the emblems of their Lord and Saviour, the poor negro sharing for the first and last time in the consecrated supper. Between him and the everlasting feast at the table of Christ's own providing, but a few fleeting hours intervened.

As they rode home that evening, Basil Greene made inquiries concerning the two ministers he had heard, and learned something of their history. The preacher of the morning discourse was Elder David Thomas, then nearly sixty years of age, who had been a minister of great distinction in Virginia. Besides the natural endowments of a vigorous mind, and the advantages of a classical and refined education, he had a melodious and piercing voice, a pathetic address and expressive action. Such was his great and persuasive eloquence that persons frequently travelled more than a hundred miles to hear him. During the first years of his ministry he met with much persecution, being frequently assailed, both by individuals and mobs. He lived to an advanced age, and was blind for several years before his death, but his spiritual vision was never dimmed or quenched in the least.

The other was Elder Lewis Craig, one of the very first to introduce the Gospel into Kentucky, and one of the most remarkable men of the age in which he labored.

For many years he suffered persecution in Virginia, the Baptist then being a proscribed people in that State. He was frequently confined in jail as a martyr to his love of religious liberty and the rights of conscience. When imprisoned on one occasion, in Fredericksburg, he preached through the grates of his prison to large crowds. Elder Craig died old and full of honors, leaving his honorable name as a legacy to a large and influential family in Kentucky.

It was in defence of such heroic men, and such principles, that Patrick Henry delivered his speech at the Spottsylvania Court House in 1768, which was the first outburst of his trumpet tongue in behalf of the rights of man and the cardinal doctrines of the Declaration of Independence.

XXXI.

A COURTSHIP AND ITS RESULTS.

"I THINK your Scotch friend has something tender on his mind," remarked Basil one evening, as the family group was clustered about the front door watching the fire-flies, and breathing the odorous night-air that swept past them from a field of newly mown grass.

"Tender. Why he is a rough-fisted, tough-hearted Scot. Do you suppose people of that sort have feelings?" responded Dobson, blowing a cloud of smoke from his nostrils, while the words came limping from between his lips.

"Well, if he be a Scot, or what, I care not; a man of more heart, of truer, tenderer, braver feelings, cannot be found," said Mrs. Burkitt, for she was still mindful of the great and good heart that had prompted him to peril his own life to rescue hers, and she would not allow anything to be said in disparagement of her noble preserver.

"Oh! I understand you, Basil;" and then Mrs. Hardy, in a most confiding manner, detailed how Campbell had for months past, ever since the days of the Sugar-camp, been particularly attentive to the widow Janes, and had even, she believed, gone so far as to make a proposal of marriage.

"Yes, such is the fact," said Basil. "When I mentioned the other day, in his presence, my contemplated departure for Lexington, he called me aside and whispered a wish, that I would not leave until after a certain thing happened. To-day, as I was riding by his school-house, he hailed me, and said that Thursday night was the time fixed—that, in fact, it was to be his wedding night, and he desired I should stand up with him."

"Why, the wretch! To be married Thursday night and not one word said to me about it!" blurted out the indignant Madam Hardy.

"Aw, but there's time enough yet," spoke a broad voice in the shadow. It was the subject of their confidential chat, who had thus come suddenly upon them out of the silence of the night.

" Well, I heard a part of your conversation. I suppose, good friends, you approve of my intent. Matrimony is a Scriptural institution, and my wife, that is to be, is, as you know, a good thrifty woman, besides, she has had experience."

"Yes, yes," said Dobson. "You are perfectly right. The widow has had experience. Then she's a lonely woman, living down the Creek with only three negroes, and she needs some one to take care of her broad bottom lands. You'll be snugly fixed, and I reckon will give up your school, and pay more attention to your theological studies. But what will the widow say to your Scotch Presbyterianism?"

" Can't tell, indeed; but, as one of your axioms says, let us not count the chickens before they are hatched. I only came to say to you all, come over Thursday."

"Of course we shall be there. But come, sit down and smoke a last bachelor pipe with us. The widow may not like tobacco, and exercise her wifely authority in interdicting your use of the Virginia weed.

" Cannot sit to-night. Must be off."

And away he tramped, his great figure vanishing in the dark.

It was even so. The Scotch schoolmaster was about to marry an attractive widow—attractive from the size of her possessions—a widow who had persistently heretofore refused all advances toward a matrimonial alliance. Her husband was engaged in the bloody and disastrous battle of the Blue Licks, and from that ill-starred field had never returned to cheer his wife. But, from some inexplicable cause, she had taken up the idea, that he had escaped the fearful massacre, and would yet return. Many years had elapsed, and still he came not. But she was not daunted, and scorned the approach of any one who she supposed thought of occupying the place of her dear John in her affections. Notwithstanding all this, the shrewd, practical eloquence of Campbell, his national perseverance in pressing home upon her the great question, in season and out of season, finally caused the widow to yield her fond hopes to his fonder desires, and the troth was made. Any one but a Scot would have failed in such an enterprise; but the sons of Caledonia—whether it is in winning a wife or a fortune, in capturing a battery or demolishing a postulate,—never say die. They are always successful.

The eventful Thursday night arrived. The wedding guests were assembled. Dobson had attired himself in a suit of black, of antique pattern; the very same which he had obtained when he made his first appearance at the great University of Edinburgh, to enter upon his course in the "humanities." It was a little worn, and somewhat too scant for his newly-developed muscles, but, nevertheless, shone in striking contrast with the buckskin breeches and linsey hunting-shirts of most of the guests. Mrs. Janes had carefully preserved her first bridal garments through all the years of her pioneer travails and adventures, and these were donned once more to do honor to her second appearance at the altar.

Bride and groom and their attendants were standing in the midst of the room; the clergyman had just been handed the license, and the throng of spectators were on tip-toe peering over one another's shoulders to see that Gordian knot tied, which alone Death or the Chancellor can untie.

The first affirmative response, with its broad Scotch accent, had barely escaped from the groom, when crack went a rifle shot, echoing through the woods.

"That's John's gun," exclaimed the intended bride. With a bound as light as a liberated fawn, she rushed to the door, oversetting two or three of the guests in her headlong speed.

Marching through the yard, with his rifle and a coon dangling across his shoulder, was the long-lost husband.

He was duly introduced to the persons present by the overjoyed wife, who was, indeed, now no longer a widow. The occasion of the assemblage was explained, with many protestations, on the part of Mrs. Janes, of her having been faithful so long, and only yielding finally because the sawney, as she denominated Campbell, would have teased the very life out of her in a month longer."

"Well, I reckon, Molly, your supper needn't spile, if you have lost a new husband."

This suggestion was hailed with unmistakable delight by all present, and they were soon seated about the plentifully-heaped board. John took the lead in eating, as he did in talking. His long disappearance, he accounted for most satisfactorily. He had been wounded in the battle, and from the loss of blood was unable to flee with the other fugitives, so that the Indians had easily made him a captive. When the conflict was over, the red-skins counted their slain, and buried them with the usual customs and ceremonies of their tribes. They then counted the whites who had been killed, and finding that they were not so numerous as their own dead, they ranged the captives on a log, and proceeded to butcher them in cold blood. Luckily John Janes was in the exact middle of the row of prisoners, and having killed the requisite number when they reached him, he was spared. During the first years of his captivity he had suffered a thousand deaths, but subsequently, having proven tractable, he was treated with more leniency, and adopted into a chief's family as a son.

"As a son-in-law, I reckon," spoke out some one who had been listening to the narrative.

"Well, son-in-law or not, I was as good as married all the time that I was among the red heathen," answered John.

At this confession the waiting, watching, hoping, ever-constant Mrs. Janes uttered a piercing scream.

"Never mind, Molly. You needn't go off into hysterics. They had no licenses and no preachers out thar. But what has become of the feller you intended forgettin' me for? I should like to take a squint at him."

Where was Campbell? Long since he had disappeared. The feast and frolic had no attractions for him after the unlucky *contretemps* that had rendered him a widower, and thrown him back desolate upon the shoals of bachelordom, just as his feet were entering upon the golden shores of wedlock. Alone, feeling as if he were friendless above all men, the poor pedagogue had hastened through the woods to his gloomy quarters, and carefully folding his black garments, had deposited them in his cedar chest, with camphor and tobacco about them, so that the moths might be hindered from desecrating these melancholy sables. Perchance they may come in play on some more auspicious occasion?

Did that occasion ever come? We know that we shall be transgressing the rules of the high art of story-telling if we reveal here, *in medias res*, the fate of any of the characters involved in our plot. But at the risk of lessening the interest that might attach to any future appearance of Campbell upon this stage, we shall lift the veil from his future.

It is 1795, the year of St. Clair's defeat by the Indians in the Northwestern Territory. John Janes was engaged as a volunteer in that encounter, and with too many other brave fellows was killed. Actually and positively killed, scalped, buried, and his name reported to the War Department as one of the dead. No mistake this time. He might revisit the pale glimpses of the moon; but could never again disturb a wedding feast with his bodily presence. Even Mrs. Janes was satisfied. Campbell, who from pedagogue had risen to the pulpit, and was lashing men's consciences in place of boys' backs, again proffered his hand and heart.

Accepted. Married. Not without many misgivings on the part of Campbell. He was continually haunted with the presentiment that some sharp rifle shot would dissipate his domestic happiness, and a stalwart spectral hunter march in to assume mastery of the house and fields he had usurped.

But these were only illusive conjectures of his brain. No fleshly realities ever entered into his happy home for the purpose of producing discontent. There were children, and grandchildren, and we are bold to say, that if you will look into one of the sweetest cottages that now brightens old Mason, you will find a group of rosy-cheeked great grandchildren.

May the line, established with such difficulty, never be extinguished!

XXXII.

WE DISCUSS POLITICS.

THE stump-speech of our young Virginian, upon his advent into the county, whereof Campbell had spoken in such exalted terms, had favorably impressed many hearers besides the quiet and conservative Caledonian, and the friends of the measures then advocated by Wilkinson were alarmed at the rapidly gaining public sentiment hostile to a Spanish protectorate. They dispatched a messenger to Wilkinson at Lexington, and informed him, if he would have delegates chosen to the Danville Convention, partial to his policy, he must come down and set matters right. This warning the energetic politician did not neglect. He hastened to combat the arguments of the Union advocate, and appointed a day for the public discussion of the political condition of the county.

Even at that early period Kentuckians found their chief delight in these logomachic tournaments—these sharp and bitter contests of the intellect. Fond as they were of the chase and the Indian foray, they loved, above all things else, to cluster about some leader and hear him pour out his flood of reasoning, of wit and eloquence, upon political topics. They were all partisans and all discussed the various questions with the liveliest animation. Over their toddies they talked politics, occasionally warming until blows were exchanged. In the harvest-fields they argued. When on the hunt they beguiled the tedium of the night-watches with wordy conflicts. Every household was a debating club. The women even took an interest in these struggles, and the children shouted for the champions of their fathers' measures.

Thus it happened that the very atmosphere of Kentucky became imbued with a political cast, and that the relations of society were formed according to the bias of political sentiment. From these ancestors, who engaged with such ardor and vehemence in the strifes and canvasses and election bouts of that era, we have inherited the unexampled proclivities that now mark the Kentucky character. Everything—religion, love, business—everything save war is subsidiary in interest to the discussion and maintenance of political principles. For our side we spend breath, money and muscle; we argue and we fight; we huzza; we intrigue; we buy; we do anything, whether it is respectable or otherwise. All is fair in battle, and so in politics. Where reason fails to convince, other appliances are used. Do we see a poor devil, who would barter his suffrage for a glass of whisky, we treat him until he is blind with liquor, and then place in his shaky hand a shining half dollar that his enthusiasm may not become lessened for the want of alcoholic inspiration.

Owing to such a condition of facts, all the talent of the State, from its first settlement, has been embarked upon the treacherous and boisterous sea of politics. Hence, men able to achieve success in science, literature and art, have preferred the shouts and plaudits and votes of the crowd to the peaceful walks and shady groves and laurel crowns of scholarship. It is only when the clarion tocsin of war sounds that we forget our animosities and bickerings, and rush to a common standard to battle and bleed, brethren at once—as at the Thames and Buena Vista.

Perhaps it is well that such are the facts of history—that such is the truth concerning the Kentucky of to-day. The predominance of politics over every other pursuit has given the State an especial and peculiar character as a member of the confederacy, and has instilled into the people a spirit of patriotism so deep abiding and true that the time can never come when either of the parties would, for one moment, seriously jeopardize the safety of the Union. We may talk and threaten and gasconade. That is all for buncombe. When the hour of peril comes the heart of the populace beats true, and the captains of the opposing phalanxes know that to strike one serious blow at the Union we were born to love and cherish and defend, would be the signal for the preparation of their own death warrants. So they ground arms and shake hands and fling their banners to the breeze, each proud of the motto—"United we stand, divided we fall."

Greene was informed of the proposed visit of Wilkinson, and a deputation of the yeomanry urged him to be present and answer the speech of the distinguished soldier and politician. He pleaded, in excuse, that he was comparatively a stranger, and that it would look impertinent in one so young, and who had so recently come in the country, to thrust himself forward in an encounter with a veteran leader. But they would listen to no excuses. He must accept the challenge which had been so defiantly hurled at him, and sustain the reputation he had won in his first effort. Hardy, although opposed to the position of his guest, saw that this was an opportunity for his acquiring popularity, and exercised his influence in prevailing on him to engage in the contest. At any other time no one would have so rejoiced as Greene at an occasion of this kind. It was exactly to his humor. Above all things he loved these open tilts before the people. He knew his own resources; was confident, fluent, and had a presence that inspired respect in opponents and admiration in friends. But now he felt his mind unsettled. He was still staggering under a heavy blow. His heart was writhing with anguish. He felt his soul shrouded with gloom, and he much preferred avoiding the glare of day and the noise of crowds. At last he yielded reluctantly.

The day came on. From far and near the farmers and hunters gathered. Every path and road leading to Washington was lined with eager multitudes. No room in the town could hold one tithe of the crowd, and they assembled, as is still the custom throughout the State, in the open air.

Wilkinson was no orator; but he possessed a plain positive manner of speaking, occasionally bursting into vehemence of utterance, that could control the attention; while the apparent candor of his statements, and his frankness of explanation were as potent in winning hearts as honeyed words and graces of oratory. Cheer after cheer from lusty lungs greeted almost every sentence that he uttered, and the committee that had invited Greene wished, before the General had concluded his harangue, that they had not been so hasty. They cursed their own presumption, and trembled for the stripling who would attempt to parry blows with a disputant so stalwart and practised in the manly art of stump speaking.

Greene, however, was in no wise abashed. Whatever hesitancy he might have felt at first in confronting so formidable an opponent, had all vanished. The huzzas of the throng were musical to his ears. As the war steed hears the shock and thunder of battle, and rushes to the conflict, he heard the shout and din of the applauding concourse, and was panting for the fray. The excitement was intoxicating to his soul. His cheeks, so pale and haggard from recent illness, became flushed. His eye, dimmed by tears, brightened. His whole form, which had been shrunk and enfeebled, was in a moment filled with new life. He gave all his puny fears to the winds. There was but one thought of sadness—could Mary but have heard of this triumph and shared with him its bliss? Then, casting aside even this bitter reflection, he pushed his way toward the stand as the General was concluding, and mounted that rustic rostrum.

No word of welcome greeted his appearance; no voice of recognition was heard. He could detect no sympathizing glance in the audience. Even the friends of his policy did not dare afford him a smile of encouragement. They had been overawed by the position of the former speaker, and the tumult in his favor; but Basil was not disheartened. He knew that he could arouse the sluggish friends of Union from this torpor—

that he could charge home upon the enemy with such effect as to startle them from their sneering indifference. Without one word of apology for his seeming presumption, as he had at first intended, he began.

First, in a low, subdued tone—but with a voice so exquisitely modulated, with such clearness of articulation and words so well chosen, that each one was a keen rapier—he stated his position. He did not assail the patriotism of the distinguished advocate of a Spanish protectorate. The history of that champion he knew. His valor in the war of Independence—his sacrifices and sufferings through that long struggle had endeared him to his heart. It was the wisdom, the prudence, the policy of the measures proposed that he attacked. That vassalage to Spain, even with the right of the free navigation of the Mississippi, would be odious to freemen, he plainly demonstrated. He depicted the incongruity of language, blood and religion, and asked how could relations so intimate as had been mentioned, be sustained between nations that had no common ties—nothing but sordid, miserable avarice to bind them together. Here every blow fell with effect upon the General. His only aim in advocating his propositions was pecuniary aggrandizement. Himself a merchant largely engaged in commerce, he was already reaping golden rewards from his friendship for the Spanish, and it was plain to be seen that he advocated his policy with an eye singly to commercial prosperity. Basil excused the inefficiency of Virginia in not providing proper defences for the frontiers on the best grounds. She had just passed through the terrible Revolutionary ordeal, and while her troops were defending other portions of the confederacy, her own borders had been ravaged—her towns pillaged, and her citizens murdered by British ruffians. Since the peace, every energy had been exercised to recuperate her almost prostrate fortunes, and while she felt a mother's interest in her young child, here on the frontiers of civilization, she was too weak to extend a helping hand. But strength was again returning to her enfeebled arms. Her step was regaining its wonted vigor, and she would soon, not only as a matter of duty, but with the pride of a fond parent, place this young and vigorous athlete among the members of the confederacy—place her as a star in the diadem of freedom, and bid it shine there with a lustre that no time could dim—a star like the Julian:

> Micat inter omnes
> Julium sidus, velut inter ignes
> Luna minores.

The young orator concluded with a stirring appeal to the people. He pleaded with them for a continuance of their union with Virginia, which would ultimately result in freedom and independence as a State. He conjured them by the ties of consanguinity and affection, by the remembrance of blood mingled in a common cause, and by the hopes of a future which promised to their union blessings for themselves and their posterity to the latest times.

Wilkinson made a brief rejoinder, but he only alluded to the youth, inexperience and inconsiderate zeal of the impetuous Virginian. He said nothing by way of repelling the force of his arguments; nor did he indulge, as the listeners expected, in his usual bravado and insulting attack. He had read at a glance the character of Greene, and he saw that he was not to be browbeaten and bullied—that, if he conquered him at all, it must be by kind words, by gentle flattery, by acts of friendship. He was no opponent to meet in stern conflict, and overwhelm. A young Samson, he must be insnared by some fair Delilah and shorn of his locks and strength.

While these yeomen bold are debating the discussion over their spirits and water, let us step aside and recount, with as much historical precision as possible, the political condition of Kentucky at that period. Anarchy and discord prevailed to a dangerous degree, and the people were divided into half a dozen parties. Interest and the prospect of trade undoubtedly swayed many and reconciled them to the prospect of a union with Louisiana under the crown of Spain. General Wilkinson, Judge Sebastian and others of less notoriety, were active agents in these disgraceful intrigues. Another party was favorable to the formation of a separate and independent republic. A third was opposed to any Spanish connection, and in favor of forcing the free navigation of the Mississippi by the arms of the United States, with the invasion of Louisiana and West Florida. A fourth was in favor of soliciting France to claim a retrocession of Louisiana, and to extend her protection over Kentucky. Happily for the nation at large, the strongest party advocated a continuance of the relations with Virginia, until a separation could be peaceably effected and admission obtained into the Federal Union.

Thus distracted by conflicting factions, Kentucky passed through the years of probation; not patiently, not even hopefully—her nervous, excitable and ardent inhabitants continually agitated by the intrigues of leading citizens whose talents were devoted to schemes of personal aggrandizement and traitorous profit. That thus perplexed and thus influenced the mass of the people should, unseduced by the abilities of the leaders, remain steadfast to the doctrines of freedom and the original government, is a noble commentary on their purity and integrity and fidelity—an example that has not been lost even on this generation.

XXXIII.

MAPLE HILL ACADEMY.

CAMPBELL, after his matrimonial misadventure, went back to his school-teaching. To the Maple Hill Academy, over which he presided, suppose we go, and see how our ancestors learned—after what fashion they drank of the Pierian spring. It is preferable to go in the cool of the morning, before the sun has kissed the dewy sward, and brushed with his beamy hand the pearly tear-drops of the night from the matted grass and glossy leaves. We will cross the crooked worm fence, at the well-worn stile, and follow the beaten path through thick undergrowth, and beneath huge forest trees. Now it leads straight on, turning neither to the right nor left—anon it straggles in a zigzag manner toward all points of the compass—now turns toward the brook, and then leaves the babbling water to sing its music unheard. On, on it leads, and we tire not, for on either side the green grass seems visibly growing, the little wild flowers appear blushing into life beneath our feet, while delicate odors greet us at each step. Now comes the hill, and peering through the woody inclosure, it may be halfway to the top, we see the shrine of learning. A nearer approach reveals its diminutive proportions, and rude, unseemly appearance. While yet there is no one about, pedagogue or pupil, we will examine the structure, its architecture and the surrounding grounds.

The house is eighteen by twenty feet, built of logs, the interstices between which are chinked with a conglomeration of mud and stones. There are two apertures, one of them for a window, where the light struggles fitfully in through the oiled paper. The floor is of bare earth, and in rainy weather—for this nursery of the intellect is but ill protected from the peltings of the pitiless storm—it becomes softened with mud; measuring feet, and forming uncouth images in which, makes an interesting episode in the journey of these young wayfarers up the hill of science. The roof is formed of a layer of straw, spread over the unhewn rafters, covered by another of dirt, and followed by a third of straw. The chimney is of sticks cemented by a clayey mortar, and serves as a medium for the exit of about one-half the smoke generated by the fire, which, minus stove, fire-place, or other appendages of ordinary civilized life, is built on the floor, at one extremity of the house. The furniture is in strict accordance with the finish of the building. Two benches, formed of oak slabs, supported by cross legs, seat the pupils, while a broad board, slightly inclined, and placed against one side of the house, with proper supports, is the writing form. The teacher has a unique chair formed of hickory withes, curiously woven together, in which he places himself on a small elevation in one corner, and overlooks the assembled scholars—monarch of all he surveys.

Listen. There is a pattering of feet without, and yonder, up the path, comes a lot of urchins, gleesome and noisy as their untainted hearts can render them. By and by, a lassie struggles along, her feet bare and wet with the morning dew. And then the children from every direction make their appearance, each one bearing a load of knowledge in an armful of books, or else, in a willow basket, the noon-hour meal. Now for an hour of fun and frolic beneath these shadowy trees. All manner of gymnastics and calisthenics are practised, and upon each cheek the rose of health is blushing in glorious beauty. In every vein there courses the pure blood of life and energy, and through every system there leaps the vital current. No countenance is paled over by the hue of sickness—no frame seems tremulous or weak. One thing that these early schools taught was the free use of the limbs, and they thus diffused a litheness and activity among the pupils which has given to Kentucky her world-renowned race of men and women.

Here comes the teacher, with his staid gait, and mien of awful severity. The pupils follow, each making a low courtesy, or, as they termed it, a "kerchy." Soon commences that humming, droning sound, peculiar to all school-rooms. Then the classes are called up, and recitations in Dilworth's Spelling-book, Daboll's Arithmetic, the Columbian Orator, Morse's Geography, and the New Testament, formed the business of the day. A lesson is given in penmanship, and ever so many in ferruling.

About sun-down school breaks up, and out there bursts, into the dying sunshine, the crowd of boys and girls who, after parleying and counselling concerning their respective grievances, at last disperse homeward. The scholastic instruction of that period never went further than the list of studies we have mentioned, and five or six quarters' attendance in such a school was considered a sufficient education. The boys, upon the completion of this course, were put at the plough, or into active business. The girls entered upon a thorough training in housewifery, and beside the kitchen fire they learned to bake and broil and stew—reddened their handsome faces over the glowing coals, and in the wash-tub gave form and size to their hands. The long days passed off in the exercise of domestic drudgery, with an occasional visit to the neighbors, when knitting-needles and balls of yarn were sure accompaniments. The music of the spinning-wheel and the weaver's loom resounded in every house. And thus were educated the honest, brave, stalwart fathers and mothers of Kentucky.

XXXIV.

THE WATER-WIZARD AND HIS PHILOSOPHY.

DOBSON HARDY was something of a skeptic, uninclined to give credence to new ideas and new discoveries, and would have never been a convert to the system of Cookism, had not his family wants been such as to demand a new spring or well of water. The summer drouths rendered the neighboring branch unreliable, while every shower of rain made the water unfit for use. He was accordingly forced to test the wizard spell of Mr. Cook, who, for some time, had been travelling through the country, discovering springs by the aid of a hazel twig.

Upon invitation, and with the expectation of receiving a considerable fee, Cook visited the Hardy farm. He was quite a philosopher, and, after the fashion of that tribe, a wise-visaged, fluent-tongued man. Magnetism was his hobby, and from the lodestone he deduced a series of laws which were to regulate the moral and physical relations of men. He was but a forerunner of the wondrous wise men and women of to-day, who, with a grain of wheat in their bushel of chaff, are instituting new gospels and revolutionizing the economy of the entire world. Of course he was a self confident, strong-willed man, for trust-in-yourself is the basis of this sort of people's operations.

But we must not forget the wants of Hardy, and the manner in which Mr. Cook supplied them. The supercilious little fellow came dashing in one morning, and said that he was ready to make the discovery. Eager to witness his mode, the entire family follow the wizard, who, plucking a small forked rod, makes use of no incantations, but proceeds to soliloquize aloud, apparently indifferent as to who hears him, but all the while watching the impression that his verbose and high sounding talk has upon the unschooled listeners.

" The secret, inexplicable laws of polarity puzzled Sir Isaac Newton, and it is not to be wondered that the illiterate should be puzzled at the magnetic influence which causes a tender forked rod to vibrate and tend to the object of search in the hands of an impressed practitioner.

"There are three premises I shall lay down. These are: 1. The mind must be strongly impressed with, and in a constant state of inquiry after the thing or substance sought for. 2. The forked rod must be of a young, quick and tender growth, porous and lively; the bark being fresh and green and easy of penetration. 3. It is required to be granted, that like substances, qualities or properties have an attractive influence one upon the other.

"Now, of what does the animal frame consist; how has it been reared up; whence has it derived its support and growth; what its diet; whence arose this diet; has not all been from the bowels of the earth, without a single exception? Well, if all vegetable matter, as well as animal, is the immediate growth and offspring of the earth, which is the common parent of all, is it not fair to conclude that all vegetable matter is also composed of the same qualities or properties that the earth itself possesses? If so, the forked rod I make use of in this process is also vegetable, and consequently partakes of the same qualities or properties that the human or animal system does.

"My mind being in a constant state of inquiry after hidden water, this constant pressure upon it spreads through and affects the whole system; operates on the nerves, on the juices, and extends to the extremities, thereby strongly impregnating the effluvia which passes through the pores of the body in common perspiration; and as the system is composed of various qualities or properties, the quality of the same kind with that on which the mind labors now becomes warm, is roused into action, and for the present governs all the rest; it being the only quality which is congenial with the strong agitations of the mind.

"Now I set out in quest of fresh water. My mind is bent down to the object; the effects of the mind flow to the extremities; the nerves, the juices, the effluvia which is perspired, all are strongly impregnated with the same inquiry. I grasp the rod closely, the warmth and dampness of the hand strike through the tender bark, and into the soft and flexible pores of the wood, and the watery qualities in the rod are now roused. The attraction of the vein of water seizes the rod.

I follow the meanderings of the vein as the rod dictates. Here is a spring of water.

"Boy, here with your pick. Mark this spot and dig."

The astonished family followed Cook while he was delivering himself of the previous soliloquy. They had narrowly watched the vibrations of the twig he held in his hand, and there, where he stood, it pointed directly to the earth.

"Now," said he, "it is necessary to ascertain how far below the surface of the earth the water is. I shall proceed."

He accordingly elevated his rod, and turning his face from the point marked, walked cautiously at right angles from the object. At a certain distance the rod again operated, turning directly to his breast. Here he made a second mark. He then measured the distance between the two points, and at that distance he said the vein of water would be struck.

"Do you ask why?" said Cook. "Let me, my friends, explain this to you on strictly philosophical and mathematical principles."

"You must grant, of course, that by the laws or powers of exhalation all rarefied vapor or effluvia are caused to ascend; and that by the laws or powers of gravitation all substances are caused to descend, or at least so to expand as to form a level and be in equilibrio."

There was no one present to question, even if it had been possible, these postulates, and he proceeded:

"Well, then if the distance between the two points is equal to the distance from the vertical point to the object, it follows that those dimensions form a right-angled plain triangle, whose legs are equal, and consequently whose acute and opposite angles will also be equal, for equal lines subtend equal angles.

"To illustrate, I will draw a figure. Here:

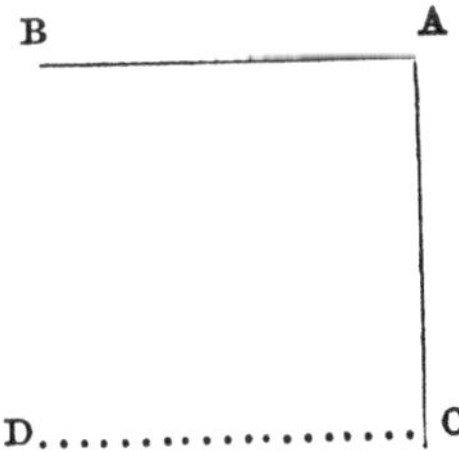

In the triangle, A B C, let C be the object, A the vertical point, B the point whence the attraction will cease to operate on the rod, and return toward the practitioner, C D, a level being parallel to A B. It is proven to a clear demonstration in the first book of Euclid that the sum of the angles in every plain triangle, as A B C, is equal to a semicircle or 180 degrees, and also that every right angle, as is the angle A, contains 90 of those degrees. It therefore follows that the sum of the other two angles B and C must also be 90 degrees; for if the three contain 180 degrees, of which the angle A contains 90 degrees, it follows that the other two, B and C, must contain the other 90. But if the line A B is equal to the line A C, it will also follow that their opposite angles, B and C, will also be equal to each other, that is, each being the equal half of 90, to wit 45 degrees.

"It is also clearly proven," continues Cook to his listeners, who by this time were clearly mystified, "in Euclid, that if two lines, as A B and C D, be drawn parallel to each other, and if a line, as B C, be drawn to intersect them, the acute and opposite angles, A B C and D C B, will be equal to each other. Hence it is inferred that the line C B exactly inclines as much to the level, C D, as to the perpendicular, C A, and no more so, but a splitting line between the two, dividing the right angle, A C D, into two equal halves of 45 degrees each. If then, as was granted at the outset, the exhaling power would cause the attractive influence of all substances to ascend and rise in the direction of the perpendicular line, A C; and if the power of gravitation would cause all attractive influences to expand, and form a level in the direction of the dotted line, C D, it follows with irresistible force that those contrary or opposing laws of nature operating at once on the attractive influence of substances beneath the surface, with equal force and power, will have a tendency to direct the rays of attraction which pass from the object to take a middle course and ascend directly with the splitting line, C B, forming angles with the level and perpendicular of 45 degrees each!"

While Cook had been thus engaged in demonstrating the truth of his theory with mathematical precision, the two negroes were testing it by a diligent appliance of spade and pick to the yielding ground. After hours of labor, within a few inches of the specified distance below the surface they struck a fine vein of water. Dobson was of course an unbeliever no longer. His incredulity gave way to implicit faith, and after that exhibition of his supposed supernatural powers, Cook could have performed anything unreasonable, and found a firm believer.

Rattling the silver with which Dobson paid him, the water conjurer rode off, elate with his new triumph, and gazed after by the wondering farm people as a sort of demigod.

We have given in detail this plan of discovering water, because it was received by all classes in the time we write of, and practised on all necessary occasions. The principles of the philosophy we have presented are submitted to this wiser and more speculative age for investigation. As a mere chronicler of what our fathers believed and how they acted, it is not in our province to decide upon so abstruse a point.

XXXV.

THE CATECHISM OF LOVE.

PLEASANT enough this holiday life in the woods and fields, which Basil Greene had been enjoying for months. Too pleasant to last, for he needs must be out in the great world, in the stirring battle, performing his part like the true man that he is. He has dallied with the flowers and loitered in the cool shades sufficiently long. He must take to the dusty high road, for the summer is going, and the flowers are dying.

Lexington was then, as it continued to be for more than a half century, the intellectual and fashionable capital of Kentucky. There had congregated, as about a common centre, the foremost men in science, war, law and merchandise.

The society was as refined as that of any of the Atlantic cities, and fashion was as potent an arbiter as in any part of the beau monde.

The talent already collected there did not daunt our young adventurer. He was the readier to enter upon a field where he could soon measure his strength, and ascertain who were his equals; for in the bold confidence of youth he did not indulge in the idea of there being any one his superior. Here, then, we have Basil Greene fairly embarked upon the ocean of life. There are favoring winds to fill his sails. His colors wear the prestige of recent victory. High-hearted, ambitious, full of genuine talent, what is there to hinder success?

Gen. Wilkinson had received him cordially, and introduced him into the most select circles, always bestowing the highest encomiums upon his genius and attainments. Not one word of the praise was wrongly bestowed. It was true, as the society in which Greene mingled soon discovered. It was gratifying to the subject, for nothing was so sweet and toothsome to him as the skillful flattery of people of position. He regarded it as corroborative evidence of his assumptions concerning himself, and was thus assured of his own correct judgment upon his own attainments.

Diligent, studious and upright, Basil had no inclination to enter the mazes of society, and would have avoided the dangers incident to the high life then prevalent in Lexington, had he not been ambitious of distinction, and eager for praise in private as in public. His earnest craving after position, and his susceptibility to flattery, rendered him weak, and though he was no fawning sycophant, the intensity of his longing for the good-will and good words of all, was a blemish, the more noticeable in one of his lofty nature. A welcome guest in the houses of all, invited to routs, parties, balls and every description of festivity, he soon became as prominent in the social ranks as at the bar, where he was rapidly attaining a leading position.

At one of these fashionable gatherings his heart, which had hitherto kept green and sacred the memory of his first love, was suddenly affected with that species of distemper for which woman is the only physician.

Lucy Connolly, who, for some months had been absent, was now returned home, and the next day after the party she could not refrain from a confidential detail of the impression which young Greene had made upon her.

"Oh, he has an air that shone like rays about his person, and no forward behavior, no studied looks, no artful posture—nature did it all. And then his eyes were so sprightly, not at all wandering, and his looks were so noble, and yet so humble; I really thought that he aimed to tell me that he could die with pride at my feet, though he scorned slavery anywhere else."

All of which girlish enthusiasm was revealed by Lucy's confidant to another confidant, and thus, embellished by each one through whom it passed, reached Basil.

That young man had been not less enthusiastic in his eulogies upon Lucy. He had eloquently praised her coal-black eyes, and the sparkling moisture and shining fluid in which they swam. He was poetical when he alluded to her dimples, where there were swarms of killing Cupids ambushed. He was amorous when he luxuriated in language concerning her lips, whose carnation dew and pouting ripeness tempted the taste. He was particularly happy, when the friend, to whom he was expatiating on Miss Connolly's charms, told him of her fortune. "Ah, yes," said he, "to borrow the language of Aimwell, in the play, Did I not read thousands in her looks? Why, she has the appearance of Ceres in her harvest: corn, wine, oil, honey, milk, gardens, groves, and purling streams played on her plenteous face."

Basil, in fact, had grown foolish. The draught of *l'elisire d'amore* had fuddled his sentiments, but sharpened his wit. He who before had gloried in trueness of heart and genuineness of intellect, was now revelling in the possibility of winning a pretty face and a well-lined pocket. He had become a worshipper of Beauty and Booty!

When next these two enamored persons met, there was scarcely the necessity of a formal introduction, so well had they learned each other's thoughts. It was a Sabbath afternoon, and Basil was on his way to church, having called, with a friend, hoping that Miss Connolly and her visitors might accompany them.

"Pshaw!" said the gay Lucy, "why go and hear David Rice? Stay with us, and I'll teach you a better catechism than the Westminster Assembly's."

"What is that?" asked both of the gentlemen.

"Well, it's the Catechism of Love; and I don't know whether Farquhar, the author, was a Scotch Presbyterian or not, but he certainly has more wisdom than all the makers of the shorter or longer catechisms. Here, Mr. Greene, sit near me, and answer as I question you."

Lucy—"What is love?"

Basil—"Love is—I know not what. It comes, I know not how; goes, I know not when."

Lucy—"Very well. You are quite an apt scholar, and must have learned this lesson of old. But tell me, sir, where does love enter?"

Basil—"Into the eyes."

Lucy—"And where go out?"

Basil—"I won't tell you."

Lucy—"What are the signs and tokens of the passion?"

Basil—"A stealing look, a stammering tongue, designs impossible and actions impracticable."

Lucy—"That's a good boy. What must a lover do to obtain a wife?"

Basil—"He must adore the person that disdains him; he must bribe the servant that betrays him, and court the person that laughs at him. He must—he must"——

Lucy—"Why, child, I must whip you, if you don't mind your lesson. He must treat his"——

Basil—"Oh, yes; he must treat his enemies with respect, his friends with indifference, and all the world with contempt. He must suffer much and fear more. He must desire much and hope little. In short, he must embrace his ruin and throw himself away."

Lucy—"Well; now tell me why Love is called a riddle?"

Basil—"Because, being blind, he leads those that see; and though a child, he governs a man."

Lucy—"Very well. And why is Love pictured blind?"

Basil—"Because the painters, out of their weakness, or the privilege of their art, choose to hide those eyes they cannot draw."

Lucy—"That's a dear, good scholar. And why should Love, that is but a child, govern a man?"

Basil—"Because a child is the end of love!"

Lucy—"And so ends Love's Catechism. Say, now, Mr. Greene, have you not learned more than you would from David Rice's sermon?"

Basil—"Yes, Lucy; and have been far happier, though I fear your teachings may result in my misery. I feel as if I had been devouring the fruit of the forbidden tree of knowledge."

This last remark was in a whisper, inaudible to the remainder of the company. The only response was a look, in which were mingled reproach, love, and all the elemental passions that blaze and burn in women's eyes.

A pretty fair beginning for a first interview.

XXXVI.

THAT THE HINDOOS WERE THE ORIGINAL INHABITANTS OF KENTUCKY.

DOBSON HARDY, who had never been any considerable distance in the interior, determined on visiting that, to him, *terra incognita.* His crops were all saved and housed, and they were glorious harvests that he had secured. The rich, new, strong land, that had been moldering and untouched by the plough for thousands of years, had yielded him a hundred fold in return for his cultivation. From among thick stumps he had gathered the golden grain, and plucked the white corn from the very borders of the dark and tangled forest. His tobacco had been cut before the first frost, and was now being cured. Concerning its disposition he must needs consult Gen. Wilkinson. He set out one clear crisp morning late in the fall; the inmates of the Hardy home sending not only kind messages, but pleasant remembrances to Basil, who still maintained his place in their hearts.

Right welcome was the honest farmer to the gaieties and pleasures of Lexington. Basil received his old friend with unfeigned satisfaction, notwithstanding his appearance reminded him of sorrows that were now well-nigh banished from his memory. Gen. Wilkinson was happy at the opportunity of purchasing the tobacco of Hardy. But happiest of all the greetings he received, was that of Pierre Savary, who, catching a glimpse of his old friend in the tavern bar-room, rushed in and embraced him with the most frantic gesticulations and the most furious torrent of words and oaths, which would have alarmed the people present had not they been some time accustomed to the demonstrative manner of the little Frenchman. It required but a moment to flood Hardy with every requisite item of information concerning his whereabouts and adventures. He had deserted the Blue Licks, and elevated himself from the position of salt-boiler to that of savan. Hardy, not knowing exactly what that was, supposed it to be some honorable trade. He had given up the common salt for the genuine Attic. Another remark lost upon the farmer.

"But come," continues Pierre, "you are just in the proper time. This evening the Kentucky Academy of Science holds its regular meeting, and I have a paper to read, proving that the Hindoos were the original inhabitants of this section of country."

Then, seizing Dobson by the arm, he hurries him off to a French café, where, instead of a rousing supper of meat and hot bread, and other strong food, he introduces him to the light and airy edibles of the Johnny Crapeaus. A number of French had lately settled in Lexington and vicinity; among them, Messieurs Duhamel, Meutelle, and Robert, gentlemen of rare scientific attainments. A Swiss colony, under the direction of M. Dufour, had also commenced the cultivation of the grape, for the purpose of making wine, near the Hickman Ferry, on the banks of the Kentucky. So these Frenchmen were not so far removed from their natural element as might be supposed. They could sip light wines, and petit verre, and drink their peculiar coffee, and be as vivacious as possible. Hardy would have been startled at the new society in which he was thrown, but having been an old campaigner in the Revolution, and fought side by side with the French, he had learned their manners, and some small fragments of their language, from the roystering and gallant troops of Lafayette. Still he was not reluctant at leaving this merry-andrew company, and when Pierre offered him a cigarette, he gave vent to all his vexation by heaping opprobrium and contumely upon a people who had no more respect for tobacco than to chop it up and roll it in nasty paper.

They reach the Academy of Science—the back room of the office of Dr. Samuel Brown, a physician of eminence, and a naturalist of rare attainments, who graduated at Edinburgh, and was a fellow of several royal scientific societies. Here, in the backwoods, he kept his enthusiasm alive for his elevated pursuits, assisted by several French gentlemen who were equally partial to similar studies and investigations.

The presiding officer on this, the occasion of Hardy's visit, was a kind of Ferdinand Fitzfossillus Felspar, who was intimately acquainted with all the internal fires and tertiary formations. He talked continuedly and learnedly, and incomprehensibly, like one of Poe's friends, about aëriforms, fluidiforms, and solidiforms; about quartz and marl; about schist and schorl; about gypsum and trap; about talc and calc; about blende and hornblende; about mica slate and pudding stone; about cyanite and lepidolite; about hæmatite and trematite; about antimony and chalcedony; about manganese and—whatever you please.

We can only afford space—to borrow an editorial expression—for a brief résumé of the very learned paper of Pierre Savary, late salt-boiler and now antiquarian. He started out with the intention of proving that the country, now known as the State of Kentucky, was originally inhabited by the Hindoos. Of course, he demonstrated this to his own satisfaction, after the following fashion:

"Not possessing the light of positive history, nor the less satisfactory glimmer of tradition, it is impossible to speak with certainty concerning the people who formerly inhabited this favored region. We are enabled, however, to construct a rational hypothesis from the relics of past ages—the debris of former civilization.

"Recent discoveries lead us to infer, with

great certainty, that we are now dwelling on the site of a once populous Hindoo empire. We infer this from the surest and only test, the analogy between the manners, customs and religion of these prior inhabitants and those of the Hindoos of the past and present.

"Within twenty miles of this place—Lexington—have been found nine murex shells. Their component parts remained unchanged, and they were every way in an excellent state of preservation. These shells, so rare in India, are highly esteemed and consecrated to their god Mehadava, who corresponds in his attributes to the Neptune of ancient Greece and Rome. This shell, among the Hindoos, forms the musical instrument of the Tritons. The foot of the Burmese god, Guadama or Budh, is represented in a statue at the capital of that empire with large feet, and the toes are carved in imitation of these shells.

"In various other places—on the farm of Gen. Kennedy and that of Mr. Jones--conch shells have been found in the ruins of circumvallatory temples, and always directly opposite to fountains. These facts lead us to no other inference, than that a people must have existed here, who placed great, we may say religious value, upon these shells.

"On Stoner's Creek, north of this, are seven piles of stone, placed in a direct line. They are from eight to ten feet high, and from twenty-five to thirty feet in diameter; the base of a circular form, and terminating in a cone at the top. These piles are situated on a commanding eminence, formed by a bluff of the creek. Such were the monuments used in ancient times by the people of Asia to commemorate important events. Then the number seven was, with the people who erected this description of monuments, a perfect number, as it is indeed with the Arabs and Hindoos to this day. Its origin is India, whence it was carried by emigrant tribes to Gothland and Scandinavia, as well as to this continent.

"Coins have also been discovered attesting the truth of this hypothesis. These were discovered on the farms of Messrs. Payne and Chambers, in this, Fayette County, and by Mr. Spear, under the root of a beech tree, on the headwaters of Bear Grass Creek, in Jefferson. The eldest bears date in the time of Antoninus, the next in the time of Commodus, the next before the elevation of Pertinax, and the last in the time of Valerian.

Coins, prior, or subsequent to the space embraced in these periods, are not found, and hence the conclusion, that they were brought into America within one or two centuries at the furthest, after the year 260, and by a people who had not afterward any intercourse with the countries in which the Roman coin circulated.

"These coins were certainly not brought here since the discovery of the continent by Columbus, for the age of the trees beneath which they were found preclude the possibility of such having been the case. Neither were they brought by a Roman colony, for had any such enterprise as visiting regions so remote been entertained, some mention would have been made of it in the chronicles of the time. We are left to only one inference, which is indeed the correct one. These coins must have been brought by those who came hither by navigation from the south and east of Asia, to the western coasts of America. In the time of Antoninus, the Romans carried on war against the Persians, and hence the diffusion of their money, which was carried into Hindostan in payment for silks, and other peculiar products. Hence it was brought here, probably in ships navigated by the Japanese, who, it is well known, have sailed over the Pacific since time immemorial. From Mexico the Hindoo civilization proceeded eastward, and there can be no question as to Kentucky having once been its seat."

When Pierre had concluded, Dobson was so delighted, that he eagerly clasped the hand of his French friend. Not delighted, however, at the learning and ingenuity in inference that had been displayed, but at the termination of what he thought was a tedious bore. But he did not wound the sensitive feelings of the little savan by inquiring what all his statements amounted to, and what would be done about it if the Hindoos did live here ages and ages agone; although he really thought that it was a matter of no consequence to the then occupants of the soil, since the former inhabitants had certainly given a quit-claim to the land, by their departure to parts unknown. Had any member of the Kentucky Academy of Science of this present era—if there be such an institution—read a theoretic paper of the above character in the presence of some hard-headed agriculturists, would his hypotheses have been tolerated so politely as by Mr. Hardy. We opine that a round oath would have been sworn, to say nothing of the inward vexation of spirit.

The bottle and the pipe were passed around before the adjournment, for they were then considered indispensable to social and scientific and religious, as well as political gatherings. Doctors drank as well as politicians, and no preacher ever presumed to enter the pulpit without first seeking inspiration from this now much perverted source.

After a few sips of toddy, and a few whiffs of tobacco, the savans adjourn, and Hardy, more fatigued than if he had set forty panels of fencing, seeks his couch.

XXXVII.

EVIL DAYS COME.

"I'VE been pestered all day with that death call in my ear. I'm sure it bodes some of us no good, and I wish that Dobson was only at home. Surely he has had time enough to go to Lexington and transact all his business."

Thus remarked Mrs. Hardy, as she and her sister were sitting before the booming fire, one November night, during Dobson's absence. Then ensued, as naturally there would from the remark already quoted, a discussion upon various signs which, however trivial they might appear, exercised no small degree of influence over both men and women. The people of that day were certainly not more superstitious than those of this latter half of the nineteenth century; yet, since they believed in ghosts and signs, the spiritualist and mesmerist and psychologist of to-day would laugh at them as very absurd. Our fathers and mothers of that far past epoch did, it is true, place too much reliance in prognostics and other methods of divining the future, but theirs was only a simple, subdued, and childlike faith, involving no desecration of religion. They did not usurp the God-possessed power of revelation. They did not set up a "Gospel of beauty" in place of that perfect one of Christ. They did not dupe poor fools, and fill lunatic asylums, and play such fantastic tricks before high heaven as make the angels weep, as do the charlatan spiritual teachers of to-day.

In the good old time the utmost confidence was placed in your luck or good fortune if you picked up a pin with the head pointing toward you. Children were careful never to spill salt, for it was a sure premonition of a sound whipping. If the ear burned, some one was talking about you: pleasant things if it be the right ear—scandalous, if the left. An itching sensation in the palm of the hand denoted that strangers were to be greeted—the nose itching, that some one was coming—the foot, that you should walk on strange ground. Three lighted candles in a room betokened a wedding, so that young misses were often known to light an extra "dip" accidentally, of course. The smoky side of the fire-place was, singularly enough, in great demand when a party of young people gathered. The smoke always came to the handsomest girl in the room. Even the most sagacious farmers always followed the light and dark of the moon in planting certain species of vegetables and crops. While no one was ever known to succeed in destroying a locust thicket when it was cut in the light of the moon. It must must be done when fair Luna has veiled her face.

Of such harmless, pleasant little matters were the two sisters conversing—their minds removed from the solemn thought which first suggested their present reflections—when a heavy but faltering step upon the porch arrested their attention. Soon the door-latch was lifted, and in there came, with a ghastly, unnatural look, and a tottering walk, Dobson Hardy. He was so faint that it was some time after he had been seated, before he could ask them to call a servant for his horse, and then, with great difficulty, he explained how the night before, in crossing Licking, he had missed the ford, and narrowly escaped with his life, after being thoroughly drenched with water. The excitement, fatigue, and exposure, had entirely prostrated him, and after lying out on the bare ground the previous night, unable to find accommodations, he had travelled all day at a slow pace through the mist and sleet and cutting coldness of the drear November weather.

The medical repertory of the two women was exhausted in search of remedial agents for the fatigued Dobson. Could watchful tenderness and heartfelt prayers and the constant application of panaceas, have availed anything, the sick man would have soon been restored. But through all the night after he reached home, he tossed upon his bed in pain and sleeplessness. Days of increasing debility followed, and in a week's time, the former stout and sturdy Dobson was but an attenuated shadow, stretched helpless upon his bed.

Although his physical sufferings were unquestionably great, still it was quite evident that his prostration was occasioned by ills that were beyond the potency of human medicaments, and must be dependent for removal upon the *vis medicatrix naturæ.* There was some secret sorrow at his heart, gnawing the tenderest fibres and rudely breaking the most sacred chords. But his unmurmuring patience and the constant care he took to make no allusion to the pains that racked his body, and the anxieties that tortured his mind, prevented even those who watched most assiduously beside his couch from ascertaining what it was that preyed upon him.

But at last there was a revelation.

The gloom of December had succeeded the dreariness of November. There was not a leaf in the forest save upon the bleak, cold earth; there was not a bird—not even the chick-a-dee, with its homely little song; the winds wailed their Miserere through the bare boughs and about the black chimneys; the clouds drooped with their murky folds close to the earth; there was no sun, no brightness, no fragrance out of doors, and within, where Dobson lay patiently bearing the burden of his affliction, the atmosphere partook strangely of the depressing darkness of the season. Vainly they heaped the fire with dry logs. The flames were not so brilliant as common; the coals did not glow with their usual ruddiness, and the sparks no longer shot with glittering frolicsomeness up the chimney.

In vain did Mrs. Hardy seek to banish the contagious gloom. It affected her as it did all things, and her smiles, as she handed the sufferer the soothing draught, were but the ghosts of those lively and hopeful marks of pleasure which formerly played over her features.

There was a knock at the door, and in response to the faint "Come in!" there entered a stranger. He inquired for Mr. Hardy, and the spectral man upon the bed was pointed out. Not caring to notice how ill the poor sufferer was, nor possessed of sufficient delicacy to await an opportuuity when he would be alone, he bluntly explained his business before all present. It was what Dobson had been anticipating all along, and the expectation had affected him more seriously than anything else. The visitor was, or so represented himself, John Sharpset, agent for Dr. Connolly, of Lexington. The object of the visit was to notify Mr. Hardy that Connally had a prior claim upon the land where he was now living, having purchased a patent for that tract which was issued years before Hardy's purchase at Richmond. There was no question about this. So careless, or rather, should we say, so wickedly negligent, were the managers of the land-office business in Virginia that they had issued patents for three times the amount of land there was in Kentucky. The whole State was thus shingled over with different claims. The evil was one of the greatest from which a people ever suffered, and it has been only within the past twenty years that any titles to landed estates in Kentucky have been secure. Companies of land pirates were organized, who purchased for mere pittances old and forgotten claims, and armed with these they harassed the possessors of the soil, driving them from their homes and happy fields, after they had passed years in bringing from the original wilderness a blossoming paradise. Never was a State so cursed as was Kentucky with these land pirates. Mere speculators, they realized enormous profits from the miseries and sufferings of the honest farmers, and many proud and mighty fortunes of to-day are built upon the wreck of homes and hearthstones and happiness, the prey of these land sharks.

Connolly was an English *émigré*, and had embarked extensively in the business of purchasing land claims, thus adding largely to his original wealth. Remorseless, cruel, unfeeling, he exacted from all a strict fulfillment of the letter of the law, and Hardy knew that it would be useless to hope anything from the leniency of such a person. He only thought that some step could be taken to stay the summary execution of the claim, and that thus he might be enabled to make provision for the future. He informed the agent of Connolly that so soon as he recovered he would take steps to adjust the matter.

"And, pray, how soon will that be?" said Sharpset.

"I am in God's hands, and how can I speak certainly of a matter of life and death. I hope, however, to be about in a few weeks," responded Dobson.

"Well, sir, in God's hands or not, you must arrange to give possession by the 1st of January, and recollect you are in our hands now!"

Mrs. Hardy had a bitter speech upon her tongue's end, but was prevented giving it utterance, for after his cruel remarks Sharpset fled, and mounting his horse was soon speeding out of sight. He did not neglect casting his eye over the fertile and rolling land, which, through his agency, was about to be snatched from the industrious and honest man who had redeemed it from its primitive savageness. Even on this gloomy day it appeared enticing, and might well awaken in his miserable breast thoughts of cupidity and avarice.

Not more than an hour had elapsed since the departure of Sharpset, when a horse, riderless and wild with affright, dashed up the forest path, and in a whinnying tone seemed begging protection. There was something unusual in the appearance of the animal, and its conduct was such as to make it evident that some startling incident must have occurred thus to throw the poor dumb animal into convulsions of terror. Tom was called from the barn to take care of the horse, and he immediately pronounced it the same that the "strange gemman" was riding. Having properly provided for the animal, he and Cash started out to ascertain, if possible, the fate of the rider, for it was evident that he had been thrown. About two miles from the house, in the midst of a dense thicket, they came upon the prostrate body of Sharpset. His head was bare and the scalp removed, for it was immediately apparent that Indians had been busy with him. From a wound in the side there oozed out the purple life blood of the poor fellow. His pulse was faint and his respiration short and difficult. Only once did he open his eyes, and that was when the faithful negroes had lifted the limp and scarcely animate body from the damp ground. Careful, lest they might occasion him an increase of pain, they proceeded home; but their loud laugh and gay chatter had ceased; their buoyancy of spirits was gone; their gibes and jests were stilled. Not only respect for the wounded man prevented their indulgence in these natural outbursts of joviality so characteristic of their race, but they had a premonition of evil which bore heavily upon them. They had not mistaken. There were Indian signs, and how did they know but that at any moment they might be pierced by the bullet shot of the foe? Cautiously, silently, and with fearful misgivings they wended their way to the house. The strange load they bore between them awakened the apprehensions of the inmates so soon as they saw them approaching. The suffering, dying Sharpset was borne into the room where Dobson lay. There, where but a short time before he had stalked in all the insolence and arrogance of health and power, he was now brought—weak and helpless, finding shelter under the roof of those he was so anxious to drive out upon the cheerless world, and obtaining relief at the hands of those he was so eager to injure and ruin.

This exciting incident and the alarming intelligence that Indian tracks had been discovered, operated very injuriously upon Dobson, and those who nursed him found it impossible to calm his nervousness. Thus suddenly had come upon them an accumulation of disturbing causes. But before night their alarm was destined to be considerably increased.

The intelligence of an Indian incursion had spread rapidly through the settlement, and an immediate resort to the stations for protection, was necessary. It had been three years since the savages had committed any serious depredations, and in that long period of quiet a fancied security had been begotten, which rendered the pioneers less able than they would else have been to resist the foe. Hardy's illness was very generally known, and a number of friends, strongly armed, gathered at his house to assist in removing him and family to Kenton's station, where they would be secure. They arrived on their mission of mercy about dusk, and preparations were instantly made for the removal.

The night settled about the earth as if robing it in eternal gloom. There was not a star to illumine the dark way. Plashes of cold rain fell from the boughs of the trees which swayed before the blast. The wagon creaked mournfully as it was drawn through the miry path. Silently followed the family upon horseback. There were no voices, no sounds, nothing human to dispel the weird influence of the night scene—of the ghostly procession. It was a weary, weary way, and midnight came before they descried the glimmering light in their desired haven of repose.

But even before the little band entered the friendly portals and nestled beneath the protecting roof-trees, two of the number had found a place of refuge far removed from the cares and dangers of life, beyond the reach of savage hate, where the wretchedness of winter nights could never more affect them.

When the wagon had reached the inner yard, Mrs. Hardy, in whose bosom the head of her husband was gently pillowed, called him, but received no answer. A servant brought a light that they might the better see how to dismount, and thus was revealed the affecting spectacle. The poor man had fallen into his last sleep during the ride, and so gently, so peacefully, that his features were unchanged, and he seemed to be but at rest. Yes, he was at rest. No longer in that gentle wife's bosom, but in the breast of Abraham.

Near by, in the same wagon, lay the body of Sharpset. His face was fixed in the stern, forbidding, ghastly shape, which death implants upon some victims. His gaping wounds and harsh features contrasted vividly with the peaceful and quiet aspect of the other dead.

Utterly desolate, wholly bereft of friends, thought Mrs. Hardy concerning herself through the weary watches of that night; and when the dark, grey, blustering morn found her sitting beside the form she had loved so long and faithfully, and she remembered that she had no spot of ground she could call her own where he could be laid at rest, what a speechless, tearless agony was hers!

They fashioned two graves within bow-shot of the station, so as to render them secure from marauding savages or beasts. And there, 'almost side by side, they placed the men who but a few days before were planning prospective schemes to thwart one another. There the robber lay near the victim. Neither to do or suffer more on earth. Both—the just and the unjust—translated to the bar of God, for acquittal and conviction.

Over the pulseless, inanimate, clammy body of Dobson Hardy, tears, sincere and meaning, were shed. His family were stricken with grief that seemed almost inconsolable, and the negroes united in the lamentations for their "marster" with a feeling and pathos that was extremely touching.

And thus the good, brave, honest, upright, God-fearing man was removed, just as it seemed most important that he should live.

"L'homme propose et Dieu dispose."

XXXVIII.

THE SCOUT'S ADVENTURE.

KENTON was rejoiced at this occasion to wreak his vengeance upon the Indians, and collecting a formidable force, he immediately set out to carry into execution his purpose of exterminating the Shawnees, who were the leaders in all the inroads upon Kentucky, and who were, furthermore, supplied with arms and ammunition, as well as gold, by British emissaries.

That is a most disgraceful page in history which records the alliance of the British with the savage hordes of the Northwest. After the close of the Revolutionary war, they spent millions of dollars in inciting the Indians to attack and destroy the feeble white settlements in Kentucky, their officers frequently commanding these atrocious enterprises. Britain paid heavily for the desolation of many homes, for the murder of many pioneers; and yet who, forsooth, gainsays the Christianity of her rulers?

When the expedition reached the Indian villages on Paint River, they found them deserted. Having burned the wigwams, and scoured the surrounding country very thoroughly, there remained nothing to do but to return home. There were no horses to steal, nor growing crops to destroy, and they retraced their steps, without a single scalp as a trophy of the excursion.

Washburn and Johnston, two adventurous hunters, were not at all satisfied with this peaceable conclusion of what promised to be an exciting foray. They, therefore, determined to leave their comrades and indulge in a scout on their own responsibility. Kenton readily acquiesced in the proposition, and would have been delighted had it been possible for him to have joined them. But he was commander of the company, and it was necessary that he should conduct it back to the station where it was organized.

Two days of leisurely and cautious adventure northward brought the scouts within the vicinity of an Indian settlement. There were signs in the forest and in the cultivated fields, upon the banks of the Scioto, and in the atmosphere, which was darkened by the smoke from watch-fires, betokening this. They, of course, increased their vigilance, and the near approach of danger added to the quickness of their already wonderfully acute senses. Advancing with stealthy steps, they found themselves at dusk upon the summit of a hill overlooking a broad area of bottom land, around which the river coursed in a semicircle. There, far below, was the encampment of the foe, whose actions they could only mark, and thus infer their intentions. The plain was dotted with wigwams, from each of which the blue smoke curled gracefully through the clear air. Although it was now quite dark, they could distinguish groups of the savages wending their way toward a central lodge, where, doubtless, the council of the chiefs was being held, and preparations made for another descent upon the border settlements beyond the Ohio. The next day, that this was their purpose became more evident. Every hour there were fresh arrivals of fiercely-painted warriors, whose approach was announced by the most savage yells. Throughout the encampment were to be seen parties of young men engaged in practising with the tomahawk and bow and arrow, the rifle being only used occasionally, for they were sparing of powder and ball. The scouts witnessed these preparations from their place of safety, nourishing themselves with the jerked meat and pop-corn which they had brought with them, and quenching their thirst at a little hill-side brook. It was their purpose to remain there in hiding until the departure of the Indians, and then, having become acquainted with their destination, leave, and by forced marches reach the white settlements so as to prevent their being surprised. But an accident prevented this well-intentioned plan being put in execution. The rifle of Washburn, which was always ready cocked, slipped, and a loud report followed, reverberating through the valley and across the plain, startling the Indians, who were in the midst of some of their sports. They almost instantly descried the smoke, and a large party of warriors hurried up the hill to ascertain the cause of this sudden explosion of fire-arms. Washburn and Johnston were at once aware of the extreme danger in which this unfortnate occurrence placed them, and they immediately attempted to effect an escape. Over the hill they stole, as quietly and expeditiously as possible, only to find that they were surrounded. Every avenue of escape was cut off save on the side of the river, and there it seemed immediate death if they ventured. The beautiful stream flowed between towering precipices on either side, and when they had reached the brink there lay before them only the prospect of being dashed to pieces by attempting to descend the almost perpendicular stone wall, or capture if they remained behind. They heard the shouts and execrations of the advancing Indians. There was no time to lose in considering between the alternative of instant death or slow torture at the hands of their captors. A hunter of Kentucky never thought twice in an emergency of that character. He decided at once, and generally with great correctness. Sober second thoughts may be very excellent things, but they are untimely in predicaments like that in which our two scouts now found themselves. Just as the first of the pursuers appeared in sight, Washburn gave a hopeful look toward a jutting crag standing isolated about thirty feet from the main hill, and the idea struck him that if he could reach it he might hold the red miscreants at bay.

He pointed it out to his comrade, and the mere gesture must have been full of eloquent encouragement, for, at the instant, Johnston attempted the leap. As he did so, Washburn turned upon the advancing Indian, and, levelling his rifle, caused him to bite the dust. He then looked to see what success had crowned the perilous undertaking of his comrade. Far down the mountain steep, yet falling amid the jagged rocks, and his descent accompanied by an avalanche of dirt and stones, he saw him hurled to instant destruction before his eyes. It was now his time to make the attempt. It was a leap for life, and the failure he had just witnessed only nerved him to greater endeavor. Retreating several paces, he ran swiftly to the dizzy edge of the precipice, and then boldly leaped forward. It was but the work of a moment, but in that time the energies of his life and soul and entire being were concentrated. He passed the intervening distance, but was not yet safe. Falling heavily on the bare rock, his feet having slipped beneath him, he barely had time to grasp a small twig, the only vegetation that marked that thunder-blasted crag. Feeble and faint from his almost superhuman exertions, and bleeding from the wounds he had received by the sharp stones, he crawled to the top of his place of refuge, and a few feet below disovered a crevice where he might possibly hide himself. Hastily descending, he entered it, but it was too small to conceal his entire person. The Indians had by this time reached the opposite ledge, and were stricken with awe at the fearful leap. None of them ventured to perform the same feat, and feeling certain that it would be impossible for the fugitive to escape from his position, they reluctantly concluded to allow him the privilege of starving in his bleak eyrie. But before quitting, several shots were fired at those portions of his figure exposed, and two of these took effect in that location where Achilles was alone vulnerable—the heel. In vain did Washburn attempt to draw up his feet. By so doing he exposed his knees, and one bullet tore the flesh from off his knee pan.

But as the evening was now advancing the Indians were forced to leave their game; not, however, without great reluctance, for, although they were certain that death would speedily overtake him in his lonely and inaccessible perch, they regretted that the privilege of burning him at a slow fire would be denied them.

Washburn, when he ascertained by the receding shouts of the Indians that they had given up the pursuit, lifted his head and began to examine his present locality. It was refreshing to be relieved from his uncomfortable position, but he soon discovered that there was barely space for him to stretch his contracted limbs, and that his situation was by no means one to beget sanguine hopes for the future. On one side, the cliff descended precipitously to the river, over three hundred feet, and on the other, over one hundred into the narrow gorge where he could see the mangled body of his friend Johnston. There were no footholds upon either side whereby he could descend. Everything was grim, stern and appalling. But his heart did not sink; his spirit did not quail; hope did not for an instant desert him. With the calmness of a philosopher he glanced toward the earth so far beneath him, and thence to the sky which was arched in beauty above him. Had the daring scout been an enthusiastic devotee of Nature, he would have been filled with delight at the unapproachable loveliness of the scene spread out before him. The sun had already set, but, marking where the fiery charioteer had disappeared beneath the horizon, were trailing clouds of purple and gold. The heavens were already becoming studded with those myriad constellations that beam so lustrously on winter nights. The distant hills were bare and brown, save where the evergreens nodded before the fitful blast. Immediately beneath him the swift river rolled onward with a sad, musical murmur—its bright waters flashing with the reflection of the newly risen moon. Than the Indian encampment nothing could have been more picturesque. Huge fires burned about the outskirts of the settlement, before which the wild demons of the forest danced in infernal glee, their shouts and yells making the night hideous. The wigwams lay in the shadow peacefully. About them moved the figures of women, as fleeting as if they were spirits. But all the beauty and novelty of the scene was lost upon Washburn, as it would have been upon any of us had we been in his place. He quietly composed himself to sleep, although there was danger of his falling from the height; but, philosopher as he was, he thought if such was to be his fate, it would be better to roll off into eternity while reposing in slumber, than to be plunged headlong to destruction with his senses keenly alive to the horror of his doom. He slept as soundly through the dreary hours of that December night, as if upon his own cabin floor wrapped in buffalo robes. No dreams disturbed him. Nor did the keen and cutting cold interfere with his repose. He had long been inured to exposure. But his thoroughly-drilled sense of hearing caused him to awake at an early hour of the grey morning. The Indians were preparing for their march, and he soon discovered them filing away after their fashion, one by one, toward the south—toward Kentucky, where they could murder and burn and devastate. This was a bitter reflection; but he consoled himself with the knowledge of their absence tending to relieve him of his embarrassment. If there was any possibility of escape, he could avail himself of it without the fear of interruption. The day came slowly on, and Washburn, having satisfied his hunger with a bite of the cold meat and a few kernels of the popped corn from his buckskin pouch, began to devise ways and means to leave his lofty pinnacle. He was not, however, long left to his own thoughts. Very soon he discovered a party of squaws on the opposite ledge, armed with bows. They immediately began discharging their arrows at him, and he was compelled to hide himself in the crevice. These female savages having tired of this unprofitable sport, once more left him to the solitude of his thoughts. But presently, whiz came another arrow, and he thought that he was again to be tortured by the female archers. He had scarcely time to mutter an execration upon savage womankind, when a stone fell at his feet, around which he perceived a slender cord was tied. Eagerly looking to see whence this signal of hope came, he perceived a squaw, as he supposed, standing where his tormentors had lately disappeared. But a more searching and scrutinizing glance revealed to him the joyful fact that this female was of his own race. In her Indian garb he descried traces of white parentage, and he readily comprehended that she would afford him the means of deliverance if in her power. Quickly he grasped the thin and fragile line and drew it toward him; a stronger rope followed, and then he saw how he was to escape. The young girl uttered not a word, but watched his movements eagerly, and motioned to the gorge beneath. He understood her gestures. They dared not speak in words, lest some one might discover them. Adjusting one end of the rope securely to the crag, he let it down, but it was not sufficiently long by fifty feet. It was the only resource, however, and Washburn determined to avail himself of it, although at the imminent risk of being dashed to pieces upon the jagged rocks below. He swiftly descended, his hands burning to blisters with the intense friction, and by the time he reached the end he was compelled, through sheer exhaustion and pain, to give way, and down, down he fell, a helpless mass to the earth. For some moments he was senseless, and only revived when he felt the tender hand of his deliverer pressed upon his pulseless temple. Fain would he have kissed the very hem of her skirt and uttered his words of thankfulness, although writhing in pain, but she pressed her finger upon his lips to warn him into silence. Lifting the almost helpless scout upon his feet, the girl discovered that one of his arms hung by his side helpless, and that a leg was powerless to move. As if endowed with superhuman strength, she caught the wounded, broken-limbed man in her arms, and tottering under the heavy load, started for the river. Resting every few moments, she at length came in sight of the stream, where a little bark canoe lay moored. But as if to intercept her flight and put to shame her holy intent, she discovered a squaw bathing in the stream. Depositing her precious burden in a secure place, she hastened to join in the aquatic sports. The squaw received her with pleasure, and they sported for a while in innocent glee, but, in the midst of their diversion, she uptripped the unsuspecting Indian woman, and in a trice had gagged and bound her hand and foot. Then, laying the helpless thing on the bank, she returned for the scout.

They were soon afloat on the river—poor Washburn lying on the bottom of the canoe, and the girl plying the paddle so dextrously that the graceful little boat shot through the water. They were safe now. Her absence from the Indian village would not be noticed until night-fall, and the only person who was aware of the escape was upon the bank of the stream immovable, her mouth so securely closed that it could utter no sort of sound, and her limbs so fastened that they could not make the slightest motion.

Now for the flight. But whither? The young girl did not know, and Washburn lay helpless and unconscious. Anywhere out of the hell in which she had existed so long. Anywhere from the demons incarnate by whom she had been so long surrounded. It might be to death beneath the clear stream—it might be to lingering starvation in the drear forest. Even these were preferable to loathed captivity. And then, was there not a hope of freedom—of a restitution to friends, to home, to kindred, to civilization, and the sunshine of Christianity? It was this hope that nerved her womanly arm, naturally so weak; that animated her heart, so often faint; that thrilled her whole being.

The current is swift. The protecting night falls about them. How the keen-prowed skiff cleaves the water, leaving a track of foam in the rear! The dark woods hang over them and keep out the unwelcome rays of the winter moon. Still the arm plies its task and the brave heart bears up, while the suffering scout moans in his agony. At last he looks about him, and is bewildered by the strangeness of the scene. During the whole flight—and hours have passed—not one word has been spoken. Washburn faintly ask, "Where am I?" and is briefly answered, "We are flying," and then sinks back to his bare couch.

The grey dawn glimmers in the east, as the boat shoots from the narrow stream into one of greater width and fiercer flow. This must be the Ohio, thinks the girl, and it is fifty miles that she has fled. Thank God for so much! But the river is filled with huge cakes of floating ice, and thump, thump they go against the fragile craft. Skillfully selecting a path through the masses of ice, she heads the boat for the opposite shore, for that must be Canetucky, of which she has dreamed so much and for which she has sighed so often. But crash comes a tremendous cake, and the canoe is crushed in. In a moment Washburn is dragged upon the ice, the paddle is saved, and there the fugitives are, in the middle of the swollen Ohio. Then it is that the scout recovers in part his long-dormant faculties, but only to be aware of the critical posture of affairs, and his utter inability to render any service either to himself or the young woman. She is appalled by the danger, but does not despair. With the paddle she pushes the cake of ice, and after weary hours of toil and anxiety they land. Then she explains to Washburn where they are and how they have escaped. He sees the necessity of informing the settlements of the contemplated Indian attack, but he cannot move, and how can she, unacquainted with the country, travel alone? But the suggestion is no sooner made than she carves out a path. She does not know these woods, but she can learn them, and with a few directions, she ventures on the daring errand of mercy. It is, overland, thirty miles from the mouth of the Scioto to Kenton's station, and thither, through these trackless forests, she is bound. In a deep covert, where no one can discover him, she lays Washburn on a couch of leaves, strikes a light with the tinder, and having built a fire, starts upon the lone journey with a step as light as you, young lady of this era, ever entered a ball-room.

Good God of the pioneers, guide these bold footsteps through the tangled forests!

XXXIX.

AN APPARITION.

"LORD a' massy! I'se seen a sperrit, mammy," exclaimed a negro girl of fifteen, as she came running into the kitchen at the station where Aunt Milly was busy among the pots and kettles.

"Hush, you foolish nigger you! Ain't these woods full enough of Injins, without you trying to res'rect ghosts?"

"Well, but I did, and on my soul, I b'leve it was Miss Mary's. I reckon old mars' he's sent her back to see how mistis and all is gittin' along," continued the younger, whose trembling frame and ashy countenance betokened that something unusual had occurred to her.

"I say," said Aunt Milly, "hush your foolishness and bring me that pail o' water I sent you to the spring for half an hour ago."

"Why, mammy, I was so skeered that I dropped the pail and run like a white-head."

"You triflin' hussy! I'll give you sometin' to run for!" raising a stick to strike the girl; but she was deterred by the appearance of her child, who was evidently verging on a paroxysm of fear. Continuing in a more soothing tone of voice, she said, "Well, come now, Tildy, and show me the sperrit. I reckon I oughtn't to be afeard, sence I've fit wild beastesses and Injins out here in this howlin' wilderness."

The two then proceeded out of the gates of the fort, into the path which led from the stockade to a large clear spring. It was the dim and shadowy hour of twilight, a rather propitious hour for the appearance of apparitions in the imaginations and fears of timid people. They had not proceeded far when the girl exclaimed, "Thar! see thar!" pointing with her finger toward the two graves.

"Why child, that's only Miss Jane and Miss Susan, standing by old mars' grave."

"Shaw, I seed them: but yonder, look, look!"

Sure enough there was to be seen the outline of another female figure flitting through the woods. It approached the grave where Mrs.

Hardy and her sister were standing. The two had just turned their faces toward the station, as the apparition glided noiselessly between them. Mrs. H. looked somewhat sternly to see who had thus dared to intrude upon the sacredness of her revery beside the last resting-place of her husband.

The sternness of the look melted in an instant, as the woe-stricken, grief-laden woman recognized in the strange, unexpected appearance, the beaming eyes and the soft voice of the long-lost Mary, who, throwing her arms about her, could but cry in the very fullness of her joy, "Mother, mother!"

Mrs. Burkitt understood, intuitively, that this was her daughter from whom she had been separated since the early infancy of the child. But her lone, desolate, stricken heart revolted when she heard the endearing appellation of mother, that rightfully belonged to her, applied with such earnest fondness and soulful lovingness to another; although she knew that the girl had been reared in entire ignorance of her real parentage.

When Aunt Milly saw these exciting demonstrations she hastened to join the group, followed by Tildy, who was not yet wholly relieved from her ghostly apprehensions. The old negro united with her mistress in the glad greeting, for Miss Mary had always been her pet, and the girl, who had been a companion and playmate of the young " mistis " through her girlish days, was not backward with her rapturous embraces when she definitely ascertained that it was not a "sperrit."

Only one of the group was silent, and that was the real mother.

But the eager Mary, though wearied out by her extraordinary toils and adventures, could not tarry there. She said that she had a message for Simon Kenton, and must see him. They hastened to the station, and found the brave warrior enjoying his pipe, as peacefully as if there were no other dangers to be confronted, and the red hand of murder never again to be averted by his stalwart arm.

The message was delivered. Horsemen were dispatched through the various settlements to alarm the farmers, and to warn the stations of the contemplated attack, and a trusty company was sent to recover Washburn, who had been left opposite the mouth of the Scioto by Mary.

The heroic young woman had eat nothing since early in the morning of the previous day; but the excitement of the flight and the arduous journey through the forest had quite banished any sensations of hunger. Now that she was safe and surrounded by her kindred and friends, a faintness almost overcame the brave spirit that had so lately undergone trials and performed exploits, sufficient to have canonized her in the middle ages. The kindness of her aunt who she still regarded as her mother, was exercised to its utmost in relieving the wants of Mary. Aunt Milly prepared a sumptuous feast, warm baths were in readiness, stimulating drinks were mixed, and when she had feasted for the first time in a civilized manner for nearly two years, she was quite another being. All of her old tenderness and ingenuousness and simplicity were restored, and nestling close to Mrs. Hardy's bosom, she recounted all the troubles of her long captivity. Hers was a simple story, unembellished by rhetoric. Had we the gift of many of our brethren of the story-telling fraternity we could fill pages with the details of the girl's experiences.

When loitering upon the hill in the rear of the

pioneer calvacade on the eventful day of her disappearance, she was suddenly seized, blinded, and her voice stifled. In this condition she was dragged into a mountain gorge, and there remained until the next morning, when her captor removed the bandages from her eyes, and "Oh!" exclaimed she, "it was that hideous man who was taken at our house in Fauquier, and then was being driven off the morning we left the old home. He said that he was my father, and that he was taking me to my mother. We travelled ever so many days on foot, over the highest hills and across rapid rivers, and then came to an Indian village. But the man did not find the person he said was my mother, and he became almost crazed with madness. He raved incessantly, and finally fell into a fever, through which I watched him until he was quite recovered. Then he became more gentle, and since that time has treated me with such kindness that I never knew what to make of it."

How she had lived among the savages and how she had finally escaped, she related in her artless, confiding manner. There was one listener to whom all her words were cutting, stabbing daggers; her own mother, of whose existence the poor girl knew nothing.

Her story completed, she fell into a gentle slumber in the arms of Mrs. Hardy, and then the two women gently composed her weary limbs on a pleasant couch, where, undisturbed, she could again enjoy the delicious sleep of freedom.

It was late next morning before Mary awoke. She was, for a moment, scarcely conscious of her situation, and unable to realize that she was again safe among those who had loved her from tender babyhood until now. All had the semblance of a dream, and she was afraid to lift her eyes and look about her lest the pleasant vision of home and happiness, in which she had been indulging, might be dissipated by the sadness of a stern reality.

But she need not fear. There, bending over her, was the kind face of Mrs. Hardy, while beside the bed, her own mother was kneeling in prayer.

"Dear, dear mother!" exclaimed Mary, reaching forward to kiss and embrace her aunt.

"But Mary, love, this is your own true, real mother," said Mrs. Hardy, presenting her sister, who fell upon the girl's bosom, sobbing as if her heart would break.

Then the whole story was unfolded to the poor, wondering Mary.

"And so that was my own father, even as he said. Oh, I ought to have staid with him, and tried to have induced him to leave those dreadful Indians. Now he is with them again, and they are coming here to try and murder you all."

What reply could they dare make to this? None. Mary was left to her thoughts and her yearnings for the safety of the father she had never regarded as such, and to the delight of her assured freedom.

And in all this time had there been no mention of Basil Greene, her betrothed lover? Yes, indeed. His praises were on their tongues continually, and her bosom throbbed with sensations that had been foreign to that maidenly temple of purity for so long and so dreary a season.

Throughout the night the people had been flocking to the station for protection, and Kenton placed himself at the head of a trusty force, determined not to await the coming of the enemy, but to march out and chastise them. At Logan's Gap, where it was most likely they would attempt to cross the Ohio, he prepared an ambuscade. Nor was he any too soon. The Indians, several hundred strong, marched up cautiously just at nightfall, intending, doubtless, to make their attack under the shadow of night. They were allowed to proceed some distance in a narrow gorge leading to the river, when the word was given, and the fifty ambushed riflemen discharged their death-dealing volley. Every man had selected his mark, and not a shot was fired amiss. Each told with deadly effect upon the red-skins. Before they could recover from the consternation into which this sudden attack had thrown them, the riflemen had reloaded their pieces and discharged them with the same fatal precision as before. The Indians were unable to withstand these disastrous blows from a hidden foe. An hundred of their warriors lay dead or in the agonies of death, and the remainder fled in every direction. Pursuit would have been vain, and the hunters, well satisfied with their exploit, rushed among the slain to secure the scalp-locks. While they were busily engaged at this bloody work, Kenton observed one of the men strike, with the stock of his gun, a person who was attempting to rise. He thought that he discerned the features of a white man, although they were disfigured with daubs of paint. Just as the keen knife was entering the scalp he begged the man to desist, and questioning the prostrate foe, he ascertained that his surmises were correct, and that he was a white. He further inquired as to the reason of his presence among the Indians, and the man responded, that he had been taken captive years before, and was forced to engage in their undertakings or be murdered.

The story was not a very plausible one, but Kenton thought that it would be best to convey him to the station, and there investigate the matter further. He accordingly acted.

Elate with their success and flushed with victory, the troops returned home, only regretting that they had missed the main body of Indians, who had gone another route, and intended attacking the settlements near and beyond the Kentucky River.

On the ensuing day Mrs. Hardy, hearing that there was a wounded stranger in the station, visited him. The recognition was mutual instantly. It was Burkitt. But she said nothing; only alleviated his sufferings and administered to his wants, as far as was in her power. She then sought out Kenton, and confided to him the exact and full particulars of her knowledge concerning his wounded guest, but begged him never to whisper one word of what she detailed. Doubtless the miserable man had suffered enough, and from appearances death would soon efface all memory of his manifold transgressions. Besides, an exposure would entail needless suffering and disgrace upon the wife and daughter.

Kenton listened with interest to the narrative of Mrs. Hardy; not, however, without indignation at some portions, displaying the mendacity of Burkitt. But he acquiesced in her wishes, for the sake of the daughter, whose heroism had won for her the admiration of all hearts.

Mrs. Burkitt and Mary were apprised of the presence of the husband and father, and they regularly visited the now delirious sufferer. Not one word was breathed concerning the man. These four kept their own sad secret closely locked in their bosoms. He was faithfully tended, and for weeks lingered on the very brink of eternity. But the warm days of the spring revived his prostrate frame, and he was finally able to totter about the house and yard. He was never again the stout, muscular man of former times, and affliction seemed to have subdued the harsh and repulsive features of his face, while his brain, that had so long and so actively plotted wickedness, was quite paralyzed, and Burkitt, the strong, hearty, bold man of old, became a feeble, drivelling idiot.

XL.

PERPLEXED.

BASIL GREENE had just completed a very elaborate toilet, and was seated before the blazing wood fire in his bachelor apartment, rubbing his hands and smiling to himself with a self-satisfied sufficiency of manner, that rendered it evident that his lines had fallen in very pleasant places. Nor need we wonder at the eloquent and famous young attorney. He has most excellent cause for his present complacency of mood. He is on the very threshold of the golden realm. Before him are years of sunshine. The shadows are all in the background. The beaker of happiness is prepared for his lips, and it must be a long, long time before the dregs are reached, if ever they do pollute his taste. He casts his eye about him, and the happy dog sneers at the bald and bare appearance of the chamber, though it is a snug and cozy place to indulge in idle dreams and puff the pipe of unwedded peace. But he sneers and wonders that he has been content so long in this forlorn condition. And then he stirs the fire anew, and the flames flash, and the sparks sparkle, and the coals candesce; and he sees a beautiful vision, which he would have embalmed in immortal verse or on glowing canvas, had he possessed the genius of that doubly-gifted poet-artist—our *cher ami*—Brannan, who sings thus of one of his own day-dreams:

" Dark tresses clung about her neck
In such a captivating guise,
As would have made another wreck
Of Adam and his Paradise;
But saving grace was in her eyes.

" No Venus rising from the sea,
By an immortal pencil limned,
Could show such loveliness as she;
All praise that poets ever hymned
Her virgin purity had dimmed.

" The peach-bloom blushed upon her cheek,
The lily paled upon her breast,
The love-light shone from eyes as meek
As ever soothed a soul's unrest:
I blest her as my angel guest."

This rare and radiant vision appeared to Basil as he gazed into the fire, but he had neither skill of pen or pencil to retain even the shadow of this form divinely fair. Nor need he. Had not he and the reality of that maiden meek vowed never more to part,

> "And sealed the vow on lip and cheek?"

The truth is, Lucy Connolly, who had catechised Basil concerning love, taught him to feel the tender passion, and there resulted, as is, we believe, the common custom, a betrothal between the two young people. And this was to be the night of their union. Hence the brilliant costume of Basil and the luxurious fantasies in which he was indulging.

The door opens, and Sam, a shining-faced negro, enters with a package of letters and papers, for this was the evening on which the bi-weekly post from the Ohio River arrived. At that period the postal service of the West was very limited, and as late as 1799, the people were content with one mail from the seaboard every three months. Basil's correspondence was chiefly with that miserable class of persons involved in lawsuits, and as he glanced over the letters he was astonished to find one superscribed in a delicate feminine hand. Opening this first, for his curiosity was instantly awakened, he glanced at the signature. As his eye rested upon a well-known name—a name that had been a charm to him in years by-gone, and the very appearance of which ever awoke strains of sad music in his heart—he shuddered as if a blast from the frosty Caucasus had swept through the room. Pale and trembling he read the brief letter:

"KENTON'S STATION.

"MY DEAR BASIL:

"I am here safe and well, as one raised from the dead, after so long and so dreadful an absence from you. I hear you praised by everybody, and am fearful that you will find one unworthy of your good and great self in your

"MARY."

There could be no mistake in this. He recognized the penmanship of Mary, and there, to confirm all, was the issue of the "Kentucke Gazette" of that week, with an account of the escape from Indian captivity of a young white woman. In looking at the paper before, he had barely noticed the caption of the article. Instinctively his eye now turned to it, and, with alternating emotions of hope and fear, he read it through. It detailed everything with a minuteness we have not attempted, and was a confirmation of the genuineness of the letter, which was "strong as proof of holy writ."

Most of us find it difficult enough to secure the affections of one young woman, and count ourselves lucky if we can but bask an occasional hour in the sunshine of some maiden's smiles. Now, here was an individual not a whit more comely than any of us unmarried and marriageable dogs, with two *care spose*, and actually in distress—perplexed with uncertainty as to his proper course of conduct—troubled with qualms of conscience, and positively quivering with fear at the near approach of the hour which was to see him united, for better for worse, with the loveliest and gentlest belle of Lexington.

Through all the mutations of his career, Basil had preserved green the memory of his early love. The lapse of time had only hallowed and rendered more sacred the remembrance of the ideal of his first passionate thoughts. His successes had been shorn of half their pleasure because Mary could not partake of the joy they had brought him. Even the brilliant beauty and fascinating manners, and tender sentiment of Lucy Connolly could not banish the winsome country girl from his recollection. He had shrined her in his heart of hearts as the holy object of his worship and idolatry. His newly-created passion had not in the least weakened the force and fervor of the old, and he had not been chary in painting her graces in the presence of Lucy. Nor was she loath to listen to his eloquent praises of the loved and lost. Doubtless, had she not regarded Mary as dead, the monster, Jealousy, would have reared his hideous head in that bosom which now swelled regularly with the undisturbed pulsations of satisfied love. In Basil's somewhat pathetic reverence for the past, she saw a guaranty of his fidelity to her in the future.

To one situated as was Basil, the revelation of Mary's existence was distressing. So exacting is womankind that it would be impossible for him to act without incurring the serious displeasure of some persons. He could not forsake Lucy, for every tick of his watch notified him of the nearer and nearer approach of the hour when he should meet her who was even now bosoming the bridal flowers

> ——"with graceful art
> Above the beatings of her heart."

And then, when he recurred to Mary, and remembered all that she had been, and pictured all that she could be to him, his heart revolted. But his fate seemed fixed. His destiny was precipitating him into the commission of what he considered a crime; the brand of traitor was ready for his brow. He again read the simple, loving words of Mary, and kissed the signature, and fondled the bit of paper over which her innocent hand had passed, and his brain was agonized with the thought that so soon he was to act a part where his heart could not be, dissemble though he might. He was thus inflicting self-torture when he heard the long-expected rap at his door. It was time for the groomsmen to appear, and these, thought he, must be my friends who are to lead me to the sacrifice.

But, instead of

> ——"a pompous traine and antick crowd
> Of young gay swearers with their lowd retinue,"

there entered General Wilkinson. He did not seat himself before beginning:

"Well, Basil, the game is up. It may be a hard blow to you, but 'there's as good fish in the sea'—you know the rest."

"Pray what do you mean, General? You speak in riddles. This is all an enigma to me."

"Enigma, is it! Well, I shall tell you the plain story, Basil, without borrowing any of your own rhetorical embellishments. Upon the body of a spy taken prisoner during the last Indian incursion were found papers proving clearly the complicity of Doctor Connolly in certain British intrigues, and his connection with the parties who are instigating the savages to their outrages upon the settlements. We informed him of the discovery, and advised him to flee with all precipitancy, lest the people should hear of his guilt, and their passions, you know, would be difficult to restrain. So Connolly has fled secretly this evening, and by this time is halfway to Limestone, where he will cross the river and escape to the more congenial clime of Canada. Before leaving, he gave me a power of attorney to settle his business, and in that capacity I pay you this visit. Here is a package for you."

Untying the cord with which the small bundle was secured, he saw a note, and read as follows:

"Basil, he is forced to fly, and it is well that it is so, and that I accompany him. You have been grossly deceived. I am not his daughter. God be thanked that I have been hindered from polluting your blameless life by a union which would have been a foul lie.

"I have begged him for the inclosed papers, hoping they may be of service to your kind friends. LUCY."

Struggling to master his emotion, Basil merely glanced at the papers, but he saw that they were the original title-deeds to the Hardy farm, and a written withdrawal of all claims to the estate on the part of Doctor Connolly.

Arising, he said, calmly:

"Suppose we walk, General?"

Arm-in-arm, the two proceeded down the dark, unpaved street to the tavern where the usual crowd of tippling gossippers had gathered. The flight of Connolly was already bruited about, and formed the staple of all conversation. So there was nothing enticing in that, and Basil, disengaging himself from his companion, returned to his solitary room.

While he is thoughtfully wending his way back, let us state the whole truth concerning this Doctor Connally; for General Wilkinson only gave the version that best suited him. He was not apt ever to criminate himself. The facts of history are these: Connally had been a British agent at Fort Pitt during the Revolutionary war, and was subsequently an emissary of the Earl of Dorchester. Under the pretext of closing up some old, unsettled business, and searching for confiscated lands, he came to Kentucky, but his real business was that of a secret agent of the Governor-General of Canada, to arrange with some of the leading men of the State for a return to British protection and an invasion of Louisiana. Privy to all his purposes, objects and schemes were General Wilkinson, Colonel Marshall, and Colonel J. Campbell. To what an extent of guilt they were involved it is not in the province of this chronicler to say.

Whether to be perfectly happy or entirely miserable, Basil could scarcely determine. Fate, which seemed just before so implacable, had removed the only obstacle to the consummation of his earliest desires, and he was now about to quarrel with it for depriving him of Lucy. Her goodness, grace, and gentleness were magnified tenfold to his vision, now that she was gone forever from his possession.

He tossed for hours upon his bed, and when he slept he clasped to his breast Lucy, but to awake and find himself the cheated victim of an illusive dream. At last there hovered near his pillow a figure clad in more than angelic purity and radiance. It gently clasped his hand and led him through groves fruit-laden, where all the way was primrosed; where heaven unfolded its azure, checkered with snowy fleeces; where the air was all spice and every bush a garland wore. Then uniting him to Mary, the good angel promised the twain

"Sweet, downie thoughts, soft lily shades, calm streams,
Joys full and true,
Fresh, spicie mornings and eternal beams."

XLI.

CLEARING UP.

IT was sixty miles from Lexington to Kenton's station, over a rough path, scarcely worthy, even at that period, of being styled a road. Two or three days were most usually occupied in performing the journey. But Basil Greene knew no weariness, and his noble horse, like that which Adonis rode,

> ———" did excel a common one
> In shape, in courage, color, pace and bone."

Fast and furious was the pace, the livelong day, and night found the hurrying rider among the well-known fields and woods where he had enjoyed his first months in Kentucky. Like an old border knight in the graceful pride and chivalry of his bearing, he presented himself at the portals of the station and demanded admittance in the name of Love, whose cavalier he was. Kenton knew the voice, and as he was sitting warder near the entrance, made him welcome, with a hearty grasp and heartful words.

"Oh no," said Simon, "they've not gone to bed yet. There's a young woman who's sick, if not dead by this time, and they are watching by her. I reckon you've come to take the folks away from the station. You needn't mind. They are, I'm sure, most welcome here."

"Well we won't talk of those things now. Please show me where I can find these friends of mine," responded Basil.

"Here this way."

It was but a few steps into the room where the sick lay, and into the embrace of Mary, who, angel as she was, had been solacing the dying hours of a pale young woman, brought there that day fatally wounded by a fall from her horse.

The entrance of Basil aroused the feeble failing faculties of the scarcely conscious sufferer, and, turning her eyes dimmed with the damps of death upon the lovers who are clasped heart to heart, and soul to soul, she faintly utters "Basil." He starts to hear his name thus whispered from the shores of death, and looking toward the bed, he recognizes Lucy. Her look in return is half-reproachful, but she beckons him to her, and he kneels at the bedside.

"Is it Mary?" she asks.

"Yes Lucy. What would you have?"

Then she calls Mary, who kneels next to Basil, and joining their hands, she lays her own delicate palms upon their heads and blesses them with her dying breath.

There needs must be mutual explanations. Mary informs Basil of the accident by which a blood-vessel was ruptured causing Lucy's death, and the fact of her companion having continued the journey, leaving the wounded woman in their care. Basil then tells Mary everything, honestly, frankly and candidly. And they are both the happier for this interchange of confidence.

XLII.

EPITHALAMIUM.

THERE only remains now for us to ring the marriage bells and sing the epithalmium. Then the book will be closed, the company must consider itself dismissed, and our pen will be converted into what, perhaps, it would have been better had it been originally shaped—a knitting-quill for our mother's behoof.

Never shone the Hardy home so fair as upon this May day. Enwreathed with trellised vines, garlanded with roses, decked with all the floral beauties of the month, it was a bower where peace and happiness dwelt, and where Love was soon to fold his purple wings, and light his torch upon the altar of wedded bliss.

The kitchen is redolent with the steam of savory stews and choice comfits, and old Aunt Milly's ivory teeth glisten with delight at the success which has crowned her preparations for the feast. Tildy is resplendent in a spick-and-span-new dress, and in her efforts to be serviceable, is constantly making mistakes. Tom and Cash, and the representatives of Young Africa, are arrayed in holiday attire.

Mrs. Hardy and Mrs. Burkitt sit together and are happiest in silence. They have had their sorrows, but to-day their cup brims with joy, and so shall it ever be for them, world without end.

The children of the household, whom we have treated with little consideration in the preceding pages—simply because they are most lovely and attractive out of books and out of company—are sporting in all the mad frolicsomeness of youth upon the green lawn.

Yonder, loitering down the well-worn forest path, is Burkitt. He knows that it is a gala occasion, and feels that his presence would not be in harmony with a scene of innocent happiness.

Above-stairs in the little attic room, with her bridesmaids grouped about her, is Mary. Theirs and hers is the bloom of youth and truth and beauty, and a pretty sight it is when they entwine

——"with merry fingers fair,
Their garlands in her sunny hair."

It is high noon, and high time that the bridegroom and the wedding guests should come. And there they are. Do you not hear the clatter of horses' hoofs over the brush-heaps and the thickly strewn logs, and the fire of that salvo away in the deep woods? And there, foremost of the chase, their steeds foaming and reeking and the riders shouting in high glee, the tall man on the tall horse wins the prize—a bottle of whisky, fixed at the gate, to be secured by the first person in the race—and as he snatches the Black Betsey, he exclaims, in a voice that we must certainly have heard before:

"Ha, ha! little Frenchy, you're no go. I'm the feller to swim with the tide and sail with the wind, to stem the torrent and weather the pint. I always come off with flyin' colors and carry the day. But here, old friend, take a swig of the creeter comfort."

Sure enough, it was Rip Snorter, Esq., and Pierre Savary, the pilots on the Ark voyage, and they were now, as then, hale fellows well met.

Weddings, in that good old time, were characterized by numerous observances abolished in these latter days. The guests were accustomed to assemble at the residence of the bridegroom, and then escort him to the home of the bride. With loud revelry and riotous glee they made the way rejoice. Nor was the path one of pleasantness. Friends generally placed obstructions across it, and there were occasional ambuscades, whence discharges of firearms would burst upon the cavalcade. The race for the bottle was the finale of the march.

It is a goodly procession as it advances up the hill, and there, in the midst of all—you can tell which is he by the graceful air with which he sits his steed—is Basil Greene. Mary, who is looking from her little window, singles him out at once, and the mad pranks and queer antics of the escort cannot win her eye from the lord of her heart.

There is a little porch wreathed with the sweet honeysuckle, and there Basil and Mary, robed in garments fit to have graced any nuptials, stand up before the man of God, and enter into those holy bonds, to have and to hold from this day forward, for better for worse, for richer for poorer, in sickness and in health, to love and to cherish, till death parts them.

As they make the sacred troth, an audible Amen runs through the group of spectators, and they all declare that Campbell has done very well, considering that this is the first ceremony he ever performed. Never will he unite truer hearts in more lasting bonds.

We will not linger at the amply provided dinner-table. Out upon the green-sward! Hear the Theologian. He has not forgotten his Horace, for, with a cheery voice, he sings out:

> "Nunc est bibendum, nunc pede libero,
> Pulsanda tellus, nunc Saliaribus
> Ornare pulvinar deorum
> Tempus erat dapibus, sodales."

Ah, Campbell, hadst thou belonged to the Ebenezer Presbytery in this more pious age, thou wouldst have been excommunicated or exorcised, or exterminated.

But it was given him to live in a freer and happier time, and no wonder he sings: "Now is the time for drinking and dancing, oh, companions!"

The sports are continued out of doors until after dusk, when the music and merriment is transferred to the house. A committee of maidens then escort the bride to her chamber, and disrobe her of the garb of maidenhood. A similar committee of males perform the same office for the bridegroom.

Still with flying feet the gay guests chase the hours, until the morrow's sun appears.

And all this night there encamps about the house the angelic hosts of Love, Content, and Hope. May it be theirs to watch well these, and all other happy hearts, ever and ever!

THE END.

www.ingramcontent.com/pod-product-compliance
Lightning Source LLC
LaVergne TN
LVHW010228110826
845151LV00004B/1224
9781425526603